CAULDRON SPELLS

C. J. Busby

Illustrated by David Wyatt

Scholastic Canada Ltd.
Toronto New York London Auckland Sydney
Mexico City New Delhi Hong Kong Buenos Aires

In memory of Dianna Wynne Jones, my favourite author
since I first read *Eight Days of Luke* at the age of ten.

Scholastic Canada Ltd.
604 King Street West, Toronto, Ontario M5V 1E1, Canada

Scholastic Inc.
557 Broadway, New York, NY 10012, USA

Scholastic Australia Pty Limited
PO Box 579, Gosford, NSW 2250, Australia

Scholastic New Zealand Limited
Private Bag 94407, Botany, Manukau 2163, New Zealand

Scholastic Children's Books
Euston House, 24 Eversholt Street, London NW1 1DB, UK

www.scholastic.ca

Library and Archives Canada Cataloguing in Publication
Busby, Cecilia, 1966-
Cauldron spells / by C.J. Busby ; illustrated by David Wyatt. (Frogspell ; 2)
ISBN 978-1-4431-2478-2
I. Wyatt, David, 1968- II. Title. III. Series: Busby, Cecilia, 1966- . Frogspell ; 2.
PZ7.B96Ca 2013   j823'.92   C2012-908475-1

Published by arrangement with Templar Publishing Ltd.
This edition published in Canada by Scholastic Canada Ltd. in 2013.

6 5 4 3 2 1   Printed in Great Britain CP 149   13 14 15 16 17

MIX
Paper from
responsible sources
FSC® C020471

CAULDRON SPELLS

Contents

Cauldrons and Promises

I f Adolphus the dragon had not fallen through the trapdoor and landed head first in Max's cauldron, then the cauldron would not have ended up severely bent out of shape, and maybe Max's spells wouldn't have gone quite so spectacularly wrong.

He certainly wouldn't have needed to go looking for a new cauldron, and that was really what saved them all.

Max was down in the cellar of Castle Perilous, packing, and he was as nervous as a cat at a rally of wolfhounds. Tomorrow he was leaving for the castle of the icy sorceress, Morgana le Fay, to study at her summer Spell School, and he wasn't at all sure he'd survive the experience. Last time he'd seen Morgana, it was just after he'd turned her into a frog and helped foil her wicked plot to overthrow King Arthur. Max didn't think he was exactly her favourite person at the moment, and he couldn't stop thinking about what might be waiting for him at her castle in Gore. So when Adolphus catapulted through the cellar ceiling, he nearly died of fright on the spot.

"Aaaarrghh! Help! Fire! Thunder! Sorcery!" he shrieked, scrambling to the furthest corner of the cellar, before stopping and peering through the gloom at the struggle going on in front of him. Max's spell books and carefully packed bags had been knocked in all directions, and his cauldron was rocking wildly back and forth, while two large clawed feet and a blue-green scaly tail waved frantically from the top of it.

"Adolphus!" shouted Max, his fright turning to a mixture of anger and exasperation. "You dozy dragon! Look what you've done to my packing!"

"Aarrhh . . . mmphh . . . blurgh," came a muffled voice from the depths of the cauldron. Having once been turned into a frog, Max could now understand animals' speech — but he didn't need any special ability to guess that Adolphus was saying something like, "Help! Get me out!"

Just as he started to pull at the dragon's back legs, a small head appeared above him, peering through the splintered wood of the trapdoor. A small head with long dark braids and a worried expression. It was Max's younger sister Olivia, Adolphus's owner.

"Is he all right?" she asked, trying to see into the gloom.

"Mmmphh!" said Adolphus loudly, at the sound of her voice, and swished his tail enthusiastically, whacking Max across the head and sending him flying.

"Oops!" said Olivia, as she saw Max sprawling on the straw next to a pile of upturned boxes. "I'd better come down."

A few minutes later they had managed to haul Adolphus out of the cauldron. He bounded around the cellar thanking them, while Max examined his cauldron anxiously.

"What on earth were you doing?" he asked, looking up at the hole in the trapdoor.

"Um — Adolphus was hanging upside down on a roof beam, pretending to be a bat — but he fell off and went right through the trapdoor."

Max raised his eyebrows with a sigh.

"I'm really sorry about the cauldron. Is it all right?"

"Shouldn't think so," said a voice. It was Max's pet rat, Ferocious, who had poked his head out of Max's tunic and was casting a professional eye over the cauldron. "Nope. It definitely has a list to the left. And a bulge. And a few dents. Never do a decent spell again, if you ask me."

"Do you really think so?" said Max in despair. "Mum's going to kill me. I only got it last month after I burned the bottom out of my last one."

"It's not you she's going to kill, it's me," said Olivia. "Or rather . . . it's Adolphus."

They looked at the dragon, who was happily sniffing around the cellar looking for woodlice to eat. Lady Griselda Pendragon was quite mild-tempered most of the time, but Adolphus had been trying her patience lately.

"He broke her best broomstick last week," said Olivia. "And he ruined her sunshine spell for the haymaking. It rained all afternoon. We can't tell her, Max — she said he'd have to *go* if he broke anything else!"

Adolphus looked up from his search and waved his forked tail.

"Go?" he said happily. "Go where? Are we going somewhere? Can I come? What fun! Whoopee!"

Max sighed. Adolphus was totally brainless, but, along with Ferocious, he had been through quite an adventure with them. He'd helped them when Max had first discovered his unusual frogspell and accidentally turned himself, Olivia and Ferocious into frogs; he'd helped them escape from Camelot when they'd been trapped there by Max's worst enemy, Snotty Hogsbottom; and he'd helped defeat King Arthur's scheming half-sister, Morgana le Fay, who wanted the throne for herself. Max couldn't let Lady Griselda banish him. He would just have to take a bent cauldron to the Spell School in Gore.

"All right," he said. "I won't tell. We'd better clear up the mess and mend the trapdoor."

"Bad decision, you mark my words," said Ferocious darkly from the depths of Max's tunic.

But he was wrong. It was Max's decision to take the bent cauldron that probably saved his life. That, and Olivia's ongoing campaign to train as a knight.

***

Olivia's campaign had not been going well lately, as her father was still adamant that girls could not be knights. However, Sir Bertram Pendragon was feeling especially benevolent that morning. The previous day he'd had a marvellous time hunting (caught nothing, as usual, but he'd been the last knight standing at the celebratory grog-drinking contest afterwards, and that always put him in a good mood). A brief glance in the mirror had told him that his moustache was now officially the most magnificent in Castle Perilous, and quite possibly bushier than that of Sir Lionel of Leograne, who held the current record for the kingdom. And to top it all, his favourite horse, Daisy, was now fit as a fiddle and prancing around the meadow, having recovered from a sad bout of knee strain after their last jousting competition.

So when Olivia caught him in the Great Hall and begged, yet again, for the chance to train as a knight, he didn't immediately bellow, "Over my dead body!" and storm out of the castle. He sighed, sat down in the great chair by the fireplace and gestured for her to sit beside him.

"Olivia, my dear," he said. "You are my favourite daughter—"

"Your only daughter," put in Olivia.

"Well, yes, indeed. My only favourite daughter, whom I love dearly. But I'm afraid it's simply not possible. Girls are not knights. They can't fight."

"I can fight better than Max."

Sir Bertram sighed again. It was true that his son Max was a bit of a disappointment as a squire. And it was true, too, that Olivia, though two years younger, was already almost as tall, quite as strong and a lot more fierce. If she ever got any serious training, Sir Bertram thought, she'd be a total menace. But he couldn't really tell her so or there'd be no stopping her.

He put on his most serious expression and said sternly, "You are supposed to be a lady. Ladies don't fight. Nor do they push people in the duck pond. Nor do they steal a horse and win the Squire's Gallop in disguise." He tried to sound disapproving about that particular escapade, but couldn't stop a note of pride entering his voice. She really was a fearless rider, he thought. It was a pity she hadn't been a boy. But still. The rules were clear. Girls could not be knights.

"But *Father*," said Olivia, in her best wheedling voice, "you could be the first knight to break the rules. You could be the knight with the biggest moustache, the knight who can quaff the most grog in a single swallow and the only knight whose daughter is a squire."

Sir Bertram frowned at her. It was true; he rather liked breaking rules. And it was also true that it would be rather wonderful to have a magnificent moustache *and* a daughter who was training to be a knight. Should he let her have a try?

Olivia sensed his hesitation. It was the moment she'd been waiting for. It was her best chance to strike a deal.

"Father. If I can win the Squires' Challenge in September, will you promise to let me train to be a knight?"

Sir Bertram blinked. What? The Squires' Challenge? The most prestigious competition for novice squires in the kingdom? He couldn't help it; he burst out laughing so hard he nearly choked on his moustache.

"Olivia! My dear child! What an idea! You wouldn't even be allowed to enter . . ."

"Yes, I would," said Olivia, ignoring the display of mirth. "I could disguise myself as a boy. All you have to do is sign to say I haven't been training for longer than a year. Which I won't have."

"But you haven't been training at all!" said Sir Bertram, still hiccupping and spluttering. "You'll end up in the manure heap after the first bout . . ."

"Well then, you won't have to worry about me training as a knight, will you? And I promise, if you give me a chance and I fail, I'll never ever mention it again!"

This was her trump card. Olivia had been pestering Sir Bertram for three whole months, and it had all been for this moment. The moment she offered him the possibility of peace and quiet — in exchange for one chance of getting what she wanted.

It was a master plan. Sir Bertram saw a future of blessed peace, of a new, demure and ladylike Olivia, and he took the bait instantly. After all, there was less likelihood of Olivia winning the Squires' Challenge than there was of the castle duck pond freezing over in August. And if by some miracle she did it — well, she really would deserve to be trained.

"Done!" he said, and they shook hands on it. Olivia was almost fizzing with excitement. The first stage of her plan was complete. Now she only had to get the second stage sorted and she was on her way to being a knight!

Secrets and Plans

The morning Max was to set off for Castle Gore was grey, cold and rainy. Max looked out of his window and shrugged. The weather looked as dismal as he felt. He had three days of hard riding with Sir Boris the Most Boring Knight in Christendom, and then he would be stuck in the cold misty lakeland of Gore, in the forbidding castle of Lady Morgana le Fay, for six whole weeks, trying not to get himself turned into anything unpleasant.

Sir Bertram had made it clear that if he wanted to learn magic when he came back, he would have to get his Certificate of Spell Mastery at the end of the course. But getting that would be almost as difficult as coming home in one piece. Lady Morgana had been sweet as honey when she awarded Max the prize of a place at her Spell School, but he wasn't fooled. The kingdom's most powerful sorceress had a definite grudge against him, and just thinking about her hard, pale blue eyes and her tinkling icicle laugh made him want to hide under the bedclothes and miss the trip north altogether.

He trudged to the stable to get his horse, Arnold, saddled up and ready to go, wishing that Olivia and Adolphus were coming with him. But Sir Bertram had flatly refused to let her go, and Max didn't think even Olivia was going to be able to get around him.

"Hey, Arnold," he said gloomily as he opened the stable door.

Arnold blew a friendly horsey sort of greeting that sounded a bit like, "Aha, oats on their way then?" and shook his mane. As Max emptied a few buckets of oats into the trough, Olivia poked her head around the corner.

"All packed then, Max? Got everything?"

"Yeah, I think so . . ." said Max, looking around at his assorted bags.

Olivia sidled in and asked nonchalantly, "So, did you ever get around to brewing up any more frogspell antidote?"

Max frowned at her. She was clearly trying to make her enquiry look totally innocent, but she was failing utterly. "Why would I want frogspell antidote?"

"Oh, I don't know," said Olivia airily. "Just, well, you never know. What if you meet an enchanted frog you don't fancy kissing? Or turn yourself into a frog and then can't turn back?"

Max narrowed his eyes. What was Olivia up to? She wasn't planning anything silly, was she? He glanced at his small pack of spell stuff and saw the two potion bottles poking out of one side. Just to be on the safe side, he took them out and checked. Yes — there was the frogspell, nearly a full bottle of blue gunk he'd brewed up just last month, and the newly brewed green antidote. None was missing and he knew Olivia couldn't make it herself, so it looked like she was just playing some game or other. He shrugged.

"Yes, I've got them both. So I guess if things get too bad in Gore I can always turn myself into a frog and hop home. Should only take me — oh — about three hundred years to get back. But I suppose at least I'd be alive."

Olivia looked sympathetic. "It'll be all right, Max," she said. "You'll be fine. You'll get the certificate; you're really good at spells. And then we only have to get me through the Squires' Challenge and we'll both be doing what we want!"

Max laughed. Olivia had told him the previous day about the promise she'd extracted from Sir

Bertram. "Olivia," he said. "You do know that you've got less chance of winning than Adolphus has of being awarded the prize for Brainiest Dragon in the Kingdom? You're very good, for a girl, but you've only trained with me, and I'm not exactly the world's best sword master."

"No, you're pretty much the world's worst," agreed Olivia happily. "But that's okay, Max, because I have a plan . . ." and she tapped the side of her nose with her finger and looked mysterious.

Max wondered what the plan was. Did it have anything to do with her strange interest in the frogspell? He was just about to ask, when they were both distracted by the sudden appearance of a small, white fluttering bird, which swooped through the stable door and hovered in front of him expectantly. Ferocious poked his head out of Max's tunic, impressed.

"Well, well, Max, it's a swift, for you. You're going up in the world!"

Olivia's eyes widened. A swift was a magical

note. Neither she nor Max had ever received one before, although they had seen a few — Lady Griselda occasionally used them for really important messages. Max reached out, and the swift fluttered down and crumpled into a small folded piece of creamy white parchment in his hand. He opened it. The message was addressed to him and written in a clear, firm hand. Max read it aloud.

Dear Max,
I am sure you are feeling a little apprehensive about your forthcoming visit to the castle of a certain lady. Please do not worry. I have a good friend who will be at the castle keeping a close eye out for you, and besides, I shall be there myself for the final week. King Arthur is making an official visit to his northern borders and will be staying at Gore. The lady will be anxious that nothing should happen to prevent this visit, certainly not any

mysterious or suspicious accidents to one of her young novices. So be of good heart! And, if you can, keep your eyes and ears open. I fear she is plotting something for Arthur's visit but I cannot find out what, and the king, as usual, will hear nothing against his half-sister. If you need me urgently, this swift has one more journey in it, and will find me wherever I am.

Merlin

As Max read, the message faded, and he was left with a blank piece of parchment, quivering slightly as if ready to leave immediately. Max knew that, thrown into the air with a few simple words, it would turn back into the white bird and soar off to wherever Merlin was to be found. He folded it carefully, stowed it in his belt pouch and then looked up at Olivia.

"Well!" she said, solemnly. "Merlin!"

Max felt rather similar. Merlin! He thought of

Merlin's bright, hawk-like eyes and his lean brown face. With his dark clothes and long sword, he looked like any other hardened knight, one of King Arthur's many battle-weary fighting men. But he was the most powerful magician the kingdom had ever known. And he had sent a magical message to Max! Not only that, but he had asked him to keep an eye on Morgana le Fay, and given him the means to contact him if he needed to. Max suddenly felt considerably less small and scared about the trip to Gore. He was actually starting to feel a trickle of excitement.

"Well, that's all very well, I'm sure," said Ferocious, cleaning his whiskers, apparently unimpressed. "Good to have Merlin on our side, of course. But who is this friend, exactly? And Merlin's not coming till the final week, is he? Still have to make sure we don't get chopped into small pieces before then."

Max grinned. "Oh come on, Ferocious. He seems pretty sure she won't try anything. She wants Arthur to come and visit. She doesn't want anyone suspecting she's an evil old hag, does she?"

"Well, that's what he says," sniffed Ferocious. "We'll just have to hope he's right."

"Ferocious, it's *Merlin* we're talking about here. He probably knows more about her than we do," said Olivia, exasperated.

"Hmm, well, that's all right then, obviously," said Ferocious. "I'll just go back to sleep. Wake me when you're in danger of being zapped into a dung beetle, Max, and I'll try and make sure the other dung beetles don't eat you." And he buried himself back in Max's tunic.

But Max refused to be downcast. Not with Merlin keeping an eye out for him. He felt as if a particularly indigestible and stodgy lump of pudding in his stomach had been dissolved with a cool bubbling drink of pure spring water. Max patted Arnold and started to saddle him up. Whatever happened, he was determined that he would discover what Morgana was up to. He was so busy thinking of how he would foil Morgana's plot, and reveal all to

Merlin when he saw him again, that he didn't notice Olivia gently remove the potion bottles from his saddlebags and replace them with two identical ones.

***

Max might have been feeling considerably happier about his trip, but there was no let-up in the rain. By the time everyone had gathered for farewells in the castle yard, they were all soaked through. Max's brown hair was plastered to his skin, his pale freckled face standing out white against his wet hair and dark clothes. Olivia, muffled in a long cloak, came out to give him a hug.

"Have a good trip, Max," she said encouragingly. And then, in a lower voice, "And keep your eyes peeled. You never know who might show up."

Max frowned at her. "All right. But I hope you're not planning anything."

But all she did was smile, and wink.

Lady Griselda squeezed Max so hard he thought he might just die before he even got to Gore and save Morgana the trouble. She wiped her tears with an already sodden handkerchief.

"Oh Max — darling — be good. Be careful. Work hard. Good luck with all your spells — and remember to wash behind your ears."

Sir Bertram clapped him heartily on the shoulder several times and brushed a hand across his eyes.

"Damned fly in my eye," he said. "Be good, Max. Take care, remember everything I've told you — and do us proud!"

Max nodded, and climbed slowly onto his horse.

Sir Boris, who had been waiting for the fond farewells to finish, raised his arm to Sir Bertram and said, "Don't worry Bertie, Max and I will have a fine old time. Can't wait to tell him all about my last quest . . . Most interesting story!"

Max grimaced at Olivia, and waved to his parents. The drawbridge was lowered, they wheeled the horses around, and the two of them clattered out of the castle gate and down the muddy track leading north.

A Traveller in Disguise

The rain continued to fall steadily on Castle Perilous, trickling down the stone walls, dripping through holes in the roof, gusting in through the windows and making the tapestries damp.

A puddle of water was spreading across the floor in a particularly damp and dark corner of the least-used turret of the castle, where Olivia was going over her plans, for the fifteenth time, with Adolphus.

"No, Adolphus. You need to have the potion bottle around *your* neck. *I'll* be a frog. Frogs don't have necks."

"Oh, okay. Yes. But if you're a frog, how will you get turned back?"

"You'll have the antidote. In the potion bottle. Around your neck."

"Oh, yes. In the bottle. Right then. But do we have to go now?" Adolphus was looking doubtfully out of the turret window at the rain falling from the sky in grey sheets, as if the gods had just emptied their bathwater on the castle. Olivia peered out and shuddered.

"Unfortunately, we do. We need to follow Max and Sir Boris, because I don't know the way to Gore and neither do you."

Olivia was dressed as a boy, in some old, dark and rather worn clothes of Max's. Strapped to her belt were Max's second-best sword, a small hunting knife and a large belt pouch. Her long dark-green dress was neatly folded on a chair in the corner, and laid forlornly across the dress were two neat dark braids of hair. Olivia looked at the braids rather regretfully for a minute, but then shrugged, and ran her fingers through her newly short hair until it looked nicely messy. Feeling in her belt pouch, she pulled out a small bottle — a bottle filled with some familiar-looking blue gunk.

I hope Max doesn't need the frogspell before we get there, she thought. He'd get a shock if he did, because she'd replaced it with a very similar-looking mixture of porridge and blackberries. She took a deep breath.

"Well, Adolphus, here goes."

She shook a small amount of gunk into her gloved hand, stowed the bottle in her pouch and then, shuddering slightly, flicked the frogspell onto her head. There was a BANG! and Olivia disappeared. In her place, looking rather dazed, was a small purple frog with red spots.

"Help!" said Adolphus. "Olivia's gone! Where's Olivia?!"

The frog rolled its eyes in exasperation.

"*Adolphus!*" it said, in Olivia's voice. "You really are the limit! It's me! It's Olivia! I used the potion to turn myself into a frog. Like we *agreed*. It's part of the plan!"

Adolphus looked at her for a minute, and then nodded and grinned happily. "Oh, yes! That's right. Good! So — you'd better climb on my back and we'll — um — well — I suppose I have to fly out of the window ... into the rain ..."

"Yes," said the frog, not looking terribly happy about the idea. "I suppose so ..."

She hopped over to Adolphus and scrambled onto his neck. It was rather difficult to work out how to hold on, what with only having webbed feet and Adolphus being covered in rather slippery scales. She teetered on his back for a minute or two, then decided to grab the leather cord she'd used to tie the potion bottle around his neck. She was only

30

just in time, as Adolphus lurched onto the window ledge, poked his head out into the rain, took a deep breath and launched himself into the air.

***

It was mid-afternoon before Lady Griselda found the note from Olivia. The rain had stopped, and a watery pale sun was attempting to shine through thin grey clouds, but most of the castle still looked rather dark, wet and gloomy. Lady Griselda was feeling unusually distracted, worried about how Max would manage up in Gore with Lady Morgana. She might be a very well-respected and important enchantress, but there was something not quite right about her. Too proud. Too cold. And just a bit too full of her own importance.

Lady Griselda sighed, ran her hands through her long red hair, and set off up the stairs. Olivia was supposed to be helping her polish the castle silver that afternoon, which meant she was almost certainly hiding in her chamber. But when Lady Griselda pushed open the door, there was no sign of Olivia. Instead, a smooth piece of parchment was laid carefully on the bed.

As Lady Griselda read it, she gasped, and turned pale. Tottering to the window, she leant out and spotted a familiar figure down in the castle yard.

"Bertram!" she shrieked. "Bertram! Come here! Olivia's gone!"

She paced up and down the room wringing her hands until Sir Bertram burst in through the door.

"Read it!" she said, gesturing to the parchment. He picked it up, frowning, and read:

Dear Mother
I have gone to Castle Gore. I want to join their squire training for the summer to get ready for the Challenge in September. And I want to be with Max. I have dressed as a boy and will just follow Max and Sir Boris to find the way. I have Adolphus to look after me so don't worry.
Love,
Olivia

"Don't worry? Don't worry?!" Lady Griselda's

voice rose to a hysterical pitch. "She's dressed as a boy! She's travelling three hundred miles north on her own with a pea-brained dragon for protection! Bertram! You have to go and fetch her back *at once!*"

"Er, well, yes, of course m'dear," said Sir Bertram soothingly. "I'll get her back in a jiffy, just wait and see."

"And what's all this about the Squires' Challenge? What on *earth* gave her the idea she could enter that? Bertram?! Is this anything to do with you?"

"Er, well . . . I may have, erm, slightly given her the impression that . . . well . . . that — er — you know — I'd really better be on my way if I'm going to catch her up. She's got quite a head start . . ."

Lady Griselda looked at him backing out of the room and put her hands on her hips.

"Bertram! This is *your fault*! Putting ideas into her head . . . Go and get her at once! Saddle up Daisy. And when you get back, we WILL be having words about this . . ."

Sir Bertram sighed, and set off for the stables, shouting for someone to bring him his armour and someone else to pack the saddlebags. He'd been looking forward to a nice peaceful evening. Bit of hog roast. Jug of grog. Some tall tales by the fireside. And now here he was, setting off to traipse halfway across the kingdom after an errant daughter. Still, it needed to be done. Who knew what Olivia would get up to otherwise? They couldn't have her all summer at Castle Gore dressed as a boy, training to be a squire. She could hurt someone. Cause no end of fuss.

***

Olivia was miles away and feeling extremely pleased with herself. She was stretched out, draped across Adolphus's back, with two froggy feet hooked firmly into the cord around his neck, soaking up the weak sunshine and keeping one eye on Max and Sir Boris, down below. Adolphus had quickly got the hang of flying high enough to be inconspicuous and was enjoying stretching his wings, soaring up on the thermals in a wide circle and then swooping back down.

"Wheee, this is fun!" he shouted. Olivia grinned. She had done it! She had escaped, just like she promised she would, and she was on her way to Gore with Max. Even better, there was a whole summer of training ahead before September, when she would compete in the Squires' Challenge. She closed her eyes and conjured up a picture of herself, slightly battered and worse for wear but definitely the clear winner — holding up the Challenge Cup triumphantly while all around the spectators cheered and stamped wildly. She could see Max, waving and punching the air, and her father, looking proud, and beside him, the tall dark figure of King Arthur, his blue eyes bright, smiling at her . . .

"Waaahhh!" shrieked Adolphus. Olivia came back to the present with a jerk as the dragon suddenly plummeted.

"What? What's wrong?" she shouted as Adolphus bucked and swung wildly to one side. She hung on desperately to the leather cord around his neck and tried not to slip.

"Adolphus! Get a grip! What's the matter?" she shrieked as they started to fall through the air. Adolphus was wailing, his wings were fluttering wildly. A dark shadow flashed across Olivia's vision, and then she saw a huge bird, talons out, beak open in a terrifying shriek of triumph, diving straight for them.

"Help! Aaaarghh! Olivia!" shouted Adolphus as they spiralled downwards.

She barely had time to blink before the bird was on them. At the last possible moment Adolphus rolled sideways and it missed by a feather, whistling down past them before pulling up and soaring around for another try.

Adolphus was upright now, flying as fast as he could in the other direction, but the bird was faster. Olivia squinted at it. It looked huge — but then, she was a frog. Now she could see it clearly, she was pretty sure it was just . . .

"Adolphus! It's just a buzzard! It's nothing you can't handle . . ."

"But it's really big!" wailed Adolphus, flapping desperately to try and go a bit faster. "It's really fierce! It wants to eat me!"

Olivia patted his neck with one foot, keeping the other firmly wrapped in the leather cord. "Adolphus, you're a dragon! It can't possibly eat you!"

"But it's got talons!" said Adolphus, looking behind him and trying to take evasive action. "It's got a really sharp beak!"

"Adolphus!" said Olivia crossly, as the bird got ready to dive again. "Pull yourself together! You've got claws — and you can breathe fire. For goodness' sake. Just breathe fire at it!"

"Oh, yes," said Adolphus, sounding relieved. "So I can. Although — it's a bit difficult when you're flying as well . . . I — er . . ."

Olivia looked behind her. The buzzard was dive-bombing them again, beady black eyes looking right

at her, the cruel curved beak open, just ready to snatch her off Adolphus's back.

"Adolphus!" she yelled. "Breath fire! Now!"

A jet of orange-yellow flames scorched past her and enveloped the surprised bird, which disappeared down through the air, flapping wildly and looking rather blackened. Olivia shrank down onto Adolphus's neck and tried not to fall off as the dragon, seriously unbalanced by his sudden act of bravery, plunged sideways. With a great effort, he finally straightened up, narrowly missing a tree, and they glided gently down. They landed by the side of a marshy pond, a few hundred yards from a rather dark and gloomy forest.

Both of them took a couple of minutes to recover, breathing deeply.

"Troll's toenails, Adolphus," said Olivia at last. "I thought I was dinner for sure. That, or splattered in pieces across the ground."

Adolphus gulped. "I'm sorry. I — it's just — it was a bit scary. It had a very sharp beak."

He looked rather shame-faced. Olivia gave him a pat.

"Never mind," she said, soothingly. "You scared it off in the end."

"I did, didn't I?" said Adolphus, cheering up and bouncing his tail. "*Whoosh!* Fire!"

"Um, the only thing is," said Olivia, looking around. "I don't suppose you have any idea where we've ended up?"

Adolphus, predictably, didn't. It was twilight before they finally gave up trying to find Max and Sir Boris, or the road north, and decided to settle down for the night in a tree at the edge of the forest. Olivia could barely see the line of the cart track nearby, winding into the forest just yards from their perch. Adolphus was fast asleep, draped over a branch, but she was still wide awake and nervously twitching at every strange sound. She thought she could hear a horse snorting, and peered anxiously through the gloom. There. It was definitely a horse. Was it Max and Sir Boris?

A last finger of red-gold sunlight filtered through the trees and picked out the figure of a lone knight, ambling along the track on a dapple-grey horse. Olivia pushed herself further into the tree and froze as the knight passed below and rode into the forest. She couldn't see past Adolphus, so she missed the sight of both the knight's truly magnificent moustache and the familiar bulk of his armour as he slumped on his sturdy grey mare.

"Blasted girl," the knight was muttering as he plodded on through the trees. "Could have been all warm and tucked up by the fire by now, nice jar of spiced grog . . . Squire training indeed! When I catch up with her it'll be six weeks of kitchen-wench training, and that's a promise!"

Kissing a Frog

The next morning dawned cold but bright.
Adolphus woke up with a jerk, and fell out of
the tree, dislodging Olivia, who landed with a splat
on top of him.

"Aaargh — where — what? What?" he yelled, and
started chasing his tail around in circles, snapping,
until he realized what it was. He stopped, and
coughed self-consciously.

"Good morning, Adolphus!" said Olivia cheerily.

"Erm . . . er . . . yes. Hello!" said Adolphus, looking slightly cross-eyed, and trying to focus on the small purple frog in front of him. She clambered up onto his back and then hooked her froggy legs into the cord around his neck.

He blinked, and thought very hard, and then remembered what was going on. Of course! It was Olivia! And they were following Max to Castle Gore. They were all going to have a fantastic adventure and do lots of breathing fire and chasing people. Yippee!

He soared into the air and started to circle upwards on warm air currents, while Olivia peered down, looking for the right road. There were rather a lot of paths and tracks and she really didn't have any idea which one to take, but so long as they kept going north, they were bound to get there eventually. Weren't they?

***

Sir Bertram woke up, with a slight sense of panic, unable to open his eyes. He had spent the night at a local inn, having failed to find Olivia, or catch up with Max and Sir Boris, and was currently lying on a small hard bed in a room upstairs. He tried again to open his eyes, and with a huge effort managed to unglue one eyelid. It was a start. He would probably catch up with Sir Boris today, and presumably Olivia too — but he'd definitely need to get out of bed quite soon. His head was hurting rather, and the light filtering in through the window shutters seemed particularly bright and strong. Sir Bertram heaved himself off the pillow and took a full blast of sunlight to the eyes. Searing pain exploded in his head and he fell back on the bed groaning.

It was all coming back to him.

He really shouldn't have got quite so friendly with the landlord last night. He should have stopped at the fourth jug of grog. But once the landlord heard that he'd won the Knight Who Can Quaff the Most Grog in a Single Swallow three times running, he'd insisted on a demonstration. And then another. Several in fact. And Sir Bertram knew from bitter experience that the earliest he could hope to have the use of his legs was midday. Dimly he remembered promising Lady Griselda that he'd have Olivia safely back in Castle Perilous by the next morning. He groaned, pulled his cloak over his head and tried to compose his excuses.

***

Sir Boris was about halfway through the tale of his thrilling visit to the castle of his second cousin twice removed by marriage, and it was only midday. He'd got to the bit where he went for a walk and met a boy who turned out to be his Aunt Gladys's son's best friend's brother. Max was trying hard to appear interested, but he was wondering how much more of the story he could take before he fell off his horse with boredom.

"Ferocious," he whispered, as they plodded on with Sir Boris droning away, "do you think if I fell off Arnold head first, I could knock myself out enough to be unconscious all the way to Gore?"

The rat considered.

"Probably not. But it would almost be worth the risk. If I have to listen to much more of Sir Boris and his fascinating relatives, I might just end up chewing my tail off for some light relief."

"All right back there?" called Sir Boris, twisting around in the saddle. "Thought I heard voices?"

"No, no," said Max, through gritted teeth. "Do go on with the story."

He glanced down at Ferocious, curled up in his belt pouch, and raised one eyebrow. The rat grinned, showing his pointy yellow teeth.

"Never mind, Max. Only another day or so of torture. And then it'll be Gore, and watching out for the lovely Lady Morgana . . . And proving to Merlin that you're his best spy. After me, of course. Should be fun!"

Max nodded, feeling cheered. It was a shame Olivia and Adolphus wouldn't be there with them. They made a good team. He wondered how they were doing back at Castle Perilous.

***

Olivia and Adolphus were nowhere near Castle Perilous, and they were quite definitely completely lost. They had followed the river roughly north (they thought) for most of the day, but there was no sign of Max, or Sir Boris, or indeed of any very clear road. They were flying over a wild and empty moor, with no trees, and no houses, and it was getting dark. Olivia was starting to feel quite worried, and Adolphus was not at all happy.

"I'm tired . . ." he wailed. "My wings hurt. And I'm cold. And I'm hungry. Can we stop now?"

"But there's nowhere to shelter," said Olivia for the tenth time. "We need to find some trees or something. There might be wild animals, and there's no wood for a fire."

But Adolphus had had enough. He crumpled to the ground in a heap of flapping wings and rolled over onto his back with his legs in the air, as Olivia jumped neatly out of the way.

"I can't . . . go . . . any . . . further," he announced,

and then flopped sideways and closed his eyes.

"Adolphus!" said Olivia crossly. "You can't just go to sleep! Get up at once! We need to at least find some bushes or something."

Adolphus rolled over and opened one eye. He sniffed. Then he sniffed again. His other eye opened and he grinned.

"Mmmm . . ." he said. "Food . . ."

And he scooped Olivia up, threw her onto his back, and went galumphing away in the direction of the extremely delicious smell he had caught wafting across the moor.

"No, Adolphus! NO! It might be anyone!" she shrieked, and tried to stop him, but she might as well have been a small child trying to stop a woolly mammoth. A few minutes later, they crashed over a ridge and saw below them a perfect sheltered spot, with a grassy bank, a small stream and a few stunted trees. A bubbling pot was sitting on the embers of a bright, warm campfire, and nearby a knight was sitting next to his tethered horse. Adolphus launched himself at the fire, and started dancing around the knight, waving his tail enthusiastically.

"Oh, yes, please, it smells delicious, we're very hungry your honour, your worship, and it's very cold and I'm fed up, and a bit of stew would be lovely, please . . ."

Olivia covered her eyes with one webbed foot while she tried desperately to hang on to Adolphus's neck-cord with the other. Most lone travellers, surprised by a bounding, hungry dragon (even a small one) in the middle of nowhere, skewered first and asked questions later. She and Adolphus were spit roast, for sure.

But she was wrong. The knight didn't draw a sword, or grab a lance, or pick up a sturdy axe. He laughed, and spread his hands, and said:

"Well, well! A dragon! My luck's in!"

Olivia took her foot away from her eyes and looked at him. Now she could see the man clearly, he didn't actually look like a knight. He was thin, and had a rather lopsided face with a long crooked nose, and worn clothes. His horse, calmly chomping grass behind him, was rather old and sway-backed, and the little bundle of possessions nearby didn't look like it contained armour or a sword. In fact, now she looked carefully, what she'd thought was a sword gleaming in the firelight turned out to be ... a harp. He was a bard!

Olivia breathed a sigh of relief. Bards were a much gentler bunch altogether than knights. And generally more well-disposed toward magic and magical creatures. Half their stories relied on dragons and spells to make the plot work. They'd be safe with a bard.

The man held out his hand to Adolphus, who sniffed it happily and then looked meaningfully at the pot of stew.

"So, you'd like some food, eh?" said the man. "I was just about to serve myself. You can join me."

He fetched a pewter bowl from his pack and ladled some stew into it, then threw a few pieces of meat down for Adolphus. Olivia slipped carefully off the dragon's neck — but not carefully enough. Before she realized what was happening, the man had her back leg between his finger and thumb, and she was dangling upside down in front of his face in a very undignified manner.

"Aaargghhh! Let me down, you pig-faced slimy slug's bottom!" she yelled, but all he heard was, "Craark! Craark!"

He put down his bowl and then gripped her more firmly in two surprisingly large hands, looking at her thoughtfully.

"Well, well. A rather odd-coloured frog. And travelling with a dragon. I think this might just be my lucky day. I think there's every chance you're a princess. It's probably worth taking the risk and giving you a nice big smacking kiss."

And before Olivia had a chance to even struggle, he had planted a firm kiss on her froggy head and . . .

WHOOSH!!!

Purple stars exploded around the campfire, and

what had been a frog was suddenly considerably taller and heavier and distinctly human, sprawled on the ground at the bard's feet looking very disgruntled.

"But . . . but . . . you're not a princess!" he said, looking extremely surprised. "You're . . . a boy! Are you a prince?"

"No," said Olivia grumpily, picking herself up off the ground. "I'm a . . . squire. My name's . . . um . . . Ned."

"But how—?"

"I got turned into a frog by . . . er . . . an evil witch. So . . . well . . . thanks, I guess."

The man stood up, and swept Olivia a deep bow.

"Caradoc the Bard at your service. Glad to be of assistance. Well, well. What excitement. Pity you weren't a princess, though. I could do with a bit of spare cash. Might not have to go traipsing all the way up to Gore."

"Gore?" said Olivia, excited. "You're going to Gore?"

"Yes. Hoping to offer my services to Sir Uriel and Lady Morgana le Fay: 'Caradoc the Bard, tales of bravery and sorcery a speciality . . . Winner of the Best Newcomer Award, Castle Emlyn Bardic Competition' . . ." He lowered his voice. "Of course, it's only open to members of the castle, so it's not very prestigious, but they won't know that, eh?" and he winked.

Olivia grinned. This was perfect. A travelling companion all the way to Gore. And she didn't even need to worry about reversing the frogspell when she got there. Well done, Adolphus!

A Fight!

Travelling with Caradoc the Bard turned out to be a much more pleasant experience than flying on Adolphus's back. For a start, Caradoc actually knew the way to Gore, which took all the worry out of it. For another, he turned out to be full of amusing stories, mostly of his disastrous performances at various bardic competitions. Caradoc, it seemed, was really quite a hopeless bard, always forgetting the end of stories or breaking his harp strings at the crucial moment. And then there was the time he'd forgotten the name of the ugly old hag in one tale and accidentally replaced it with the name of the lord of the castle's only daughter, who'd run out of the Great Hall in floods of tears.

"Yes, well, I don't recall getting paid for that one — actually, I think they threw me off the battlements . . . Lucky they were only ten feet high — and the moat was warm for the time of year . . ."

Olivia laughed. They were coming to the end of a golden afternoon, ambling gently north on Caradoc's horse, which was sturdier than it looked and quite happy to take the weight of both of them. Ahead, the road dipped down into a small copse of ancient elm trees that spread their branches right across the way, casting a deep shadow. As they passed into the cooler darkness, Olivia thought she heard a cry. The horse stopped, and twitched its ears. There!

It was definitely a shout. And the sound of clashing swords. Olivia twisted around to look at

Caradoc and was glad to find that he was not looking in the least bit afraid. He was frowning, and pulling a long knife out of his saddlebag. He urged the horse onwards, and she drew Max's second-best sword and took a deep breath as they cantered under the trees toward the sound.

* * *

Max and Sir Boris had been plodding on for what seemed like years. Max's backside felt like it would never be the same again. The only good thing was that Sir Boris had finally run out of tales to tell and was reduced to the odd cheery comment about the weather. Max was just wondering whether to eat his last hunk of bread now, or save it for later, when he realized a band of armed men was blocking the road ahead, led by a young squire on a horse.

"Halt, knights, and state your business!" came the call from the rider, as he approached them slowly. "The Warden of the Great Grimpen Mire requires all travellers to—"

Suddenly the boy stopped, peered forward and

then laughed. Max knew that laugh. He knew the tall arrogant figure on the horse, as well.

"Snotty Hogsbottom!"

"Well, if it isn't the weed Pendragon. Of course. On your way to the Spell School." He sneered, and then turned around and cantered back to the soldiers. "These two need to be escorted to the castle for questioning," he shouted. "They are dangerous outlaws. If they resist, arrest them!"

Sir Boris looked bewildered. "What on earth? What does he mean? Outlaws?"

Max groaned. "He knows we're not. But they'll chuck us in the dungeons for a week and then claim it was all a mistake. Meanwhile I'll miss the first week of Spell School. Slimy rotten scheming dung beetle!"

Sir Boris narrowed his eyes and contemplated the band of armed men approaching them, Snotty behind them. Boring he might be, but a coward Sir Boris most certainly was not.

"Right then, Max. There's only five of them and

a squire. You take the boy; I'll deal with the soldiers. Swords ready!" He drew his sword and urged his horse on toward the troop. Max gulped, and drew his sword. Ferocious poked his head out of Max's tunic.

"What? Fighting? Are you mad?!"

"I have to," said Max through gritted teeth. "Snotty is going to stop us getting to Gore otherwise, and apart from missing the Spell School, I won't be much use to Merlin stuck in a dungeon for a few weeks."

"But a sword?" said Ferocious, eyebrows raised. "You'll never hit Snotty with a sword, not when you're riding a horse! Use a bit of sense, Max. Chuck a bit of frogspell at him!"

"Ferocious — you're a genius!" said Max, relieved, and reached for his saddlebags. There it was — the almost full bottle of blue gunk.

Snotty was cantering toward them, while Sir Boris wielded his sword manfully, holding off all five of the soldiers. Max raised the potion bottle and grinned.

"Ha! Want to be a frog, Hogsbottom? Like your father? He made a very fetching one!"

Snotty blinked, and pulled up his horse, but it was too late. Max hurled a blob of blue potion straight at his face. It splattered over Snotty's forehead and trickled down into one eye, but Snotty remained very much a boy. Max gulped.

"So!" laughed Snotty. "Got it wrong this time, eh? You always were terrible at spells, Max. Must have just got lucky, the first time."

He waved his sword in the air and then brought it crashing down, right where Max's head would have been, if Arnold hadn't neatly sidestepped. Unfortunately, this meant that Max fell off, with a shout of surprise, and landed, winded, on the stony road. Snotty leapt off his horse and was standing over Max in a moment, holding his sword to Max's neck.

"Right, Pendragon. You're coming with me."

But at that moment a blur of blue-green came hurtling through the trees, and Snotty was knocked flying by a vision of claws, wings and forked tail.

"Adolphus?" cried Max, hardly able to believe his eyes. But the next second two more figures had thrown themselves into the fray and were laying about Snotty's men with energy and determination. Max saw one of the soldiers go flying, knocked over by an expert uppercut to the chin. The rather short figure that had delivered the killer punch looked extraordinarily like . . .

"Olivia!" he yelled. "What are you doing here?"

He scrambled to his feet, found his sword and went charging in to help. Unfortunately, the first thing he managed to make contact with was the top of Adolphus's head. The small dragon went down like a stone.

Sir Boris was fighting valiantly, and Olivia was managing to deliver a few useful blows alongside the tall stranger with the long knife, but now that Adolphus was out of the equation the five soldiers were gaining ground. Worse, Snotty, looking rather dazed but determined, was about to join the fight again. It looked like it was the end, but then Max heard a crashing sound, and a large knight dressed in black armour came charging down the road behind them waving his sword.

"Tally ho!" he shouted. "Unhand these travellers, you villains!"

The new knight was not only rather nifty with his sword; he was also extremely large and very fierce. It wasn't long before Snotty and the soldiers decided the odds were no longer in their favour, and beat a rapid retreat, scattering down the road and out of the wood.

There was a moment's silence, while they all gathered their breath. Adolphus crawled out from under a bush, groaning and shaking his head feebly. The new knight took a step backward as he saw the dragon.

"Adolphus?" he said, from inside his helmet.

Max and Olivia turned at the sound of his voice.

"Father?" said Max.

The knight pulled off his helmet and looked around.

"Well, I say. Found you all at last. Been riding all day looking for you. Just as well I caught up when I did, eh? What on earth's been going on?"

Luckily Sir Bertram's saddlebags were absolutely full of cakes, grog and cold meat ("Never know when you might need a little snack!"), so their explanations took place over a rather sumptuous roadside picnic. Some bits of the story were left out and others glossed over. Olivia and Max had a huddled and private conversation, which involved a lot of outrage on his part and much apologizing on hers, before two potion bottles changed hands. Sir Bertram gathered early on that as far as Caradoc was concerned, Olivia was a boy, and he decided not to reveal her secret. In fact, Sir Bertram was hatching a bit of a plan of his own.

"Well now," he said, as he happily devoured his fourth chicken leg. "It seems to me, we may as well all go on to Gore together. Not so far now, and after all, Morgana's a distant relative of mine. May as well pay her a visit now I'm so close. And there's damned fine hunting to be had in this corner of the kingdom, by all accounts."

He looked down at Olivia, and winked. "Besides, I think you could probably benefit from a bit of training, eh, young Oliv—er? If you're going to be up to the Squires' Challenge? All the squires at Gore are very well trained, I've heard . . ."

Olivia's eyes shone. "Yes! That's just what I was hoping. Brilliant!"

"That's settled then," said Sir Bertram, and took a deep pull on his bottle of grog. "I'll send a swift to your mother, let her know."

Caradoc leant over to Olivia, looking confused.

"I thought you told me your name was Ned?" he said.

"I did," said Olivia. "It is Ned. Short for Oliver."

***

Gore, when they finally got there, turned out to be surprisingly beautiful. The Great Grimpen Mire, and the swampy lakes for which it was famous, stretched

63

out to the north, but there were glimpses of blue sea to the west, while immediately around the castle was a lush green landscape of meadows, streams and wooded valleys. Beyond the distant lakes they could see mountains clear against the blue sky, and the white stone of the castle glowed in the mellow afternoon sun.

Lady Morgana le Fay, who met them when they arrived, was every bit as terrible as Max and Olivia remembered. She held out her arms and smiled but they felt as if an icy wind had just breathed down their necks.

"Welcome, welcome, my dear Bertram," she said, and her voice dripped with sweetness but her eyes stayed hard. "So you've come to stay as well. How *delightful*. I shall make sure you have the most comfortable quarters we can find. And this is . . . ?"

She turned to Olivia, who shivered, and then looked defiant.

"Er . . . well . . . my . . . er . . . Griselda's cousin's boy. Oliv—er. Came along with me to get a bit of training with your squires. If that's all right?"

Lady Morgana looked hard at Olivia.

"Indeed. The family resemblance is . . . striking. Well my dear . . . Oliver. We'll have to put you in with Max, I think. I'm sure you'll enjoy each other's company." And she laughed her icy, tinkling laugh and they both tried not to shudder.

But that night, curled up in bed with the candles glowing, warm and well fed, they were both feeling a lot more confident.

"She can't do much, with Dad here," said Olivia. "She won't want anything to go wrong before the king comes."

"No," said Max, yawning. "I reckon we'll be fine. She won't dare do anything to either of us."

But he was wrong. Lady Morgana le Fay had a very carefully organized plan for the king's visit. And it quite definitely involved something rather nasty happening to Max.

Spell School and Squire Training

Max arrived for the first lesson of the Spell School rather late, clutching his cauldron and his bag of books and spell ingredients. The room used for magic lessons was near the back of the castle, a large airy chamber with high ceilings and a stone floor. Scattered around the room were a dozen or so young apprentices, unpacking and sorting out their equipment. Max slipped into a space and glanced around at the others. To his left was a short, stocky girl with fair hair and a friendly smile, and in front of him was a boy with red hair and a very new-looking, shiny cauldron. Max looked down at his misshapen and battered cauldron and fervently hoped it would work.

"Right then, people," came a loud voice from the front of the room, and a tall, thin young wizard with a long face walked in. "My name is Aleric of Ullswater, and I am in charge of all lessons except the most advanced, where Lady Morgana le Fay will graciously condescend to teach you herself. I insist on absolute concentration and obedience in my classes. Any student who does not pay attention will be turned into an orange mushroom for the duration of the lesson."

He started to hand out jars and pots of ingredients, explaining that they would be trying out a relatively simple spell for immobility "to see how everyone does." Max crossed his fingers, conjured a fire and set to work, but as he chopped and stirred and muttered over his spell it began to look increasingly like Ferocious had been right about the cauldron. Max's potion was definitely not doing what it should. He looked at his spell book for the fifteenth time and then back at the cauldron. What should have been a bright orange bubbling mixture was currently a rather smelly, green sludge with lumps that refused to dissolve no matter how many times Max repeated the incantation.

"Having trouble, are we?" said Ferocious, poking his head out and surveying the mess with a practised eye. "Told you so."

"Shut up, Ferocious," said Max, desperately chopping an extra handful of slugs' toenails. "It's nearly right. I expect it will work, anyway, even if it doesn't look quite right."

The girl next to Max, who had told him her name was Marion, looked over at his spell and giggled. "Umm, not quite right that, I think. Maybe a bit more daffodil root?"

Max went pink, and carried on mixing. He tried

to look unconcerned as one by one the apprentices took their finished spells up to Aleric to test. As each apprentice flicked a small drop of their potion onto a bored-looking chicken on Aleric's desk, the chicken froze into immobility for a few seconds before being released by a drop of antidote. Max, trying to look nonchalant, brought his potion up last of all and carefully dripped a blob of sludge-green slime on the bird's head.

There was a pause.

The chicken blinked, then it jumped into the air, shrieked once and sprouted an extra pair of wings. It cackled loudly and looked reproachfully at Max.

"Ah ... Hmm ... Interesting," said Aleric. "Not *quite* right, young Pendragon, but ... an interesting variant. Perhaps you might like to practise that one a little in your spare time."

When Max finally got back to his room that evening, it was clear that Olivia's day had not been much better than his. She was sitting on a stool by the fire with her feet in a bucket of hot water and a wet cloth over her face. When she heard him come in, she lifted the cloth, and Max saw an assortment of bruises and a rather nasty cut just above her right eye.

"Morgana's stinking fat bully of a nephew, Mordred," she spat. "Five foot nothing and thinks he's king of the squires because his father is King of Orkney."

"And let me guess," said Max, looking at her bruises. "You decided to give him a piece of your mind."

Olivia put the cloth back over her face crossly. "I didn't do anything, Max, honest. He just likes bullying anyone who's new. He tripped me up twice, 'accidentally' threw a sack of grain at my head instead of onto the cart, and then nearly managed to slice my eyebrow off waving his sword around and showing off."

Max slumped down next to her and held out his hands to the fire. "Well, it looks like we both had a pretty terrible start. Let's hope tomorrow's a bit better."

But it wasn't. And nor was the rest of the week. Max continued to make a total idiot of himself in the magic lessons. On Tuesday, his "swift feet" spell turned the class snail into a snail the size of an elephant before Aleric rapidly returned it to normal size. Max spent all lunchtime scrubbing its slime off the floor. On Wednesday, his "lighter than air" spell turned the class block of granite into a marvellous statue of St. Petroc (Aleric decided to keep that one for his chambers), while on Thursday his "hair growth" spell left the bald stableman as bald as ever but with very hairy nostrils. ("Well, it's definitely hair, young Pendragon! Getting better!" Aleric had said, encouragingly.) Friday, however, was the last straw. Everyone had to test their invisibility potion on themselves. While the rest of the class popped satisfyingly out of sight, Max hit the ground like a felled tree, snoring loudly, and had to be carried to his room for the rest of the day to sleep off the after-effects.

Meanwhile, Olivia had spent the whole week

unsuccessfully trying to avoid Mordred. By Friday afternoon she had been dunked in the duck pond twice, had a bucket of pig swill "accidentally" dropped on her head, and spent most of that day searching for Max's second-best sword, which she eventually found propping open a small skylight in the armoury.

"Right, that's it!" she seethed as she came into their chambers waving her sword dangerously close to Max's ears. "Mordred has gone too far this time! Where's the frogspell, Max? This time tomorrow he's going to be croaking his head off in the castle dung heap . . . And when he finally gets someone to change him back, I'm going to fight him."

But Max wasn't interested in Mordred. He was busy pacing up and down doing his own seething.

"If I don't get a new cauldron, I'm finished. I may as well pack up and go home. I'm *never* getting the Spell Certificate, and I won't be a wizard, and I'll have to spend the rest of my life whacking stupid practice dummies with stupid swords!"

Olivia frowned at him. She was wondering if it

would make her feel better to just punch Max in the nose. He was pretty much wondering the same thing about her. Luckily, just then, Adolphus bounded up to them and started bouncing up and down with excitement.

"Do you need a new cauldron, Max? Do you really? Because I know just where to get one! We can go tomorrow! It'll be fun!"

They both looked down at him, speechless with amazement. Adolphus with an idea? Surely this was impossible?

"Did I hear you right, Adolphus?" said Max at last. "Did you say you knew where I could get a cauldron?"

"Yes, yes!" said Adolphus, happily. "My Great-Aunt Wilhelmina! She collects them!"

"And your Great-Aunt Wilhelmina lives where, exactly?" asked Ferocious, poking his head out of Max's belt pouch. "The Isles of the Blest? The outer reaches of the Northern Wastes?"

"No, quite close, actually," said Adolphus,

oblivious to the rat's sarcasm. "I visited her once, when I was little, with my Mum . . . She lives in a cave in the Forest of Gore. It's a really big cave and it's full of cauldrons! She's a bit mad . . . But she'll be really happy to see us. Er . . . I think so, anyway."

Max and Olivia looked at each other. This sounded more fun than another day spent failing to make spells work or getting cramps from propping up the practice dummy for everyone else to whack.

"We'll have to sneak away early," said Max, thinking about it.

"But how will we get past the guards at the gate?" said Olivia. "No one's supposed to go out without permission."

Max grinned. "I know. But we won't have to. We can go from one of the turrets. We can turn ourselves into dragons!"

"And just how are we going to do that?" said Olivia. "Your spells haven't exactly been behaving themselves lately, have they? You'll probably turn us into buckets."

"No, don't be an idiot! We've got the frogspell. All we have to do is turn ourselves into frogs, and then get Adolphus to kiss us . . . Remember — humans kiss you back to yourself, but if another animal kisses you, it changes you into one of them. So Adolphus can kiss us into dragons, and then the antidote will turn us back afterwards . . . What do you think, Ferocious? Fancy being a dragon?"

Ferocious considered. "I think I'll stay as a rat, thanks. There's always the danger you'll get Adolphus's brains along with his dragon shape, and then you'll need someone with you who can actually think."

***

While Max and Olivia were busy plotting their escape from the castle as dragons, Lady Morgana le Fay was with Sir Richard Hogsbottom, putting the final touches on their plans for the biggest wild dragon hunt the castle had ever seen.

"You can take the novices and apprentices along, as well. We'll want the whole castle out there. The more people there are, the more chance of finding this cave," she ordered.

"Indeed, your worship, my lady," agreed Sir Richard in admiring tones, bending his whole body toward her in an attempt to appear even more humble and ingratiating, his plump white hands twittering in front of him. "And my son, Adrian, will be out with the hunt as well, of course. He is fully aware of the situation . . . What supreme luck that you have found out the treasure is so close! So nearly in our grasp!"

Morgana's lips pressed together and she frowned. "But not *yet* in our grasp, Sir Richard. And until we find this wrinkled old dragon and her hoard, our plans cannot proceed. So do not fail me, Sir Richard. I *need* the Treasure of Annwn!"

Meeting
Great-Aunt Wilhelmina

Max was enjoying being a dragon. Getting used to his wings had been a bit tricky at first. They had soared down from the castle turret happily enough, but flying between the trees of Gore Forest required more skill. At one point Max had flown smack into a tree trunk and knocked himself senseless, which made Olivia laugh so much she fell off the branch she was perched on. After that they'd been a bit more cautious, although they hadn't been able to resist a fire-breathing contest that had left a whole trail of blackened and scorched oak trees in their wake. Ferocious had decided early on that, dim as Adolphus was, at least he had had a lot more practice at being a dragon — so he was perched on Adolphus's neck, rolling his eyes at their antics.

By midday they had reached a clearing deep in the forest, and it was beginning to look like they were lost.

"I thought you knew the way, Adolphus," said Max, exasperated.

"Well, yes, I do . . . I think . . . but I'm just not sure . . . Um, I think it's along this stream. But it might be up this path." The dragon hung his head, looking apologetic.

Olivia nudged him gently with her tail. "Don't worry, Adolphus. We'll stop for a bit, and then maybe it will come to you."

"I don't suppose so," put in Ferocious darkly. "Probably can't find the way back now, either.

Doomed to live out our lives in this forest. And you left the antidote back in the castle, so you'll be stuck as dragons for the rest of your lives." He twitched his whiskers and then grinned. "But look on the bright side. *I'm* still a rat."

"Oh stop moaning, Ferocious, and have a bit of bacon," said Max, opening the pack that had been slung around his dragon neck. "Actually the antidote's safely in my pack, along with the frogspell. And here Adolphus, I brought you some roasted woodlice."

They were all happily munching when there was a tremendous *CRACK!* nearby, quickly followed by the dim sound of a hunting horn in the distance.

"What?" said Olivia.

"Sshhh!" said Max.

They froze.

There was definitely someone approaching them through the forest. Slowly and carefully they backed away into the undergrowth at the side of the clearing, and listened as the sounds got closer and closer. It was a horse — or someone riding a horse —

and it sounded like there was only one. Max held his breath and tried to make himself as inconspicuous as a bright red-gold dragon can when hiding in ragged green and brown undergrowth.

The horse came crashing into the clearing, and before the man riding it had a chance to draw breath Adolphus flew out of the bush he was hiding in and started dancing around in front of him.

"Adolphus! NO!" hissed Max, but Olivia laughed.

"It's all right! It's Caradoc! He likes dragons."

The bard jumped down from his horse and bent down to Adolphus, scratching him behind his ears, just where he liked it.

"Well, well, hello there, Adolphus!" He looked up and spotted the others. "Found some friends, have you?"

Olivia wriggled out from under some creepers and bounded toward him, and Max reluctantly emerged from behind her. Caradoc surveyed the newcomers.

"Well, what a beautiful dragon," he said, looking at Olivia's shining silvery-purple scales. "And another fine young dragon," he added, as Max joined them. "Bad day for you all to be wandering around in these woods, my friends."

They turned to each other. What did he mean? Caradoc looked at them with an odd expression, and then turned away, apparently talking to his horse.

"If I were a dragon, I'd be a bit careful today, eh, Nellie?" he said, patting her on the neck. "What with the massive wild dragon hunt just set off from the castle. Quite a large number of squires, apprentices and knights combing the forest as we speak."

He got back into the saddle, and gave the horse a nudge to start moving. As he plodded out of the clearing, they heard him say, to no one in particular, "I wonder if they've come down from that old dragon cave? The one just up the mountain where the stream comes out. I hope they get back there in time to escape the hunt ..."

***

Jerome Stodmarsh was plodding along through the forest wishing very much that he wasn't Sir Richard Hogsbottom's ward. Learning to be a knight was one thing; getting dragged into various schemes to unseat King Arthur was another. It wasn't that Jerome cared two dragon's sneezes for King Arthur, but so far being part of the plots against him had meant being banished to Gore, forced to do sentry duty in the northern marches and now being stuck with Snotty combing the forest for a non-existent dragon.

"I really don't think there's a single dragon in this forest, Adrian," he complained as they came out into yet another silent, empty clearing. He could hear the noise of the main hunt a few miles away, but Snotty had insisted on them exploring the far western edges of the forest together.

Snotty turned around in the saddle and frowned at him.

"Do stop moaning, Jerome. I know this is the right place. The divining spell Lady Morgana did showed this as the most likely. And I want to be the one that finds it."

Jerome shrugged, and they wound their way further into the forest — until Snotty suddenly stopped, and held up a hand for silence.

"There's something ahead," he hissed at Jerome. They carefully dismounted, and crept forward on foot. Peering through the undergrowth, Jerome thought he saw a flash of blue-green scales, and then another, of red-gold.

He turned to Snotty, mouth open. "It's a dragon! More than one!"

Snotty shoved him out of the way for a closer look.

"I'm pretty sure the blue one is that stupid dragon that belongs to Pendragon's bratty sister ... What's he doing here? He never goes anywhere without his owners. Unless ..." He snapped his fingers. "It's them! They've turned themselves into dragons! Well that was a really clever move, Max. The day of the castle's major dragon hunt ..." For a moment he looked quite triumphant, thinking of Max and Olivia trussed up, ready for a special dragon-meat feast. But then his face fell. "We can't do anything. My lady's got plans for Pendragon. Wouldn't do to get in her way. But there's something funny going on here, that's for sure. I think we should follow them."

***

"Oh, where is it, where is it, where is it, where is it . . . ?"

Adolphus was anxiously chasing around in circles by a deep pool of water that appeared to be the source of the small stream they had been following. They were on the lower slopes of a large rocky hill reaching up out of the forest. It was the beginning of the long mountain chain that ran northwest of the castle — Max knew they were called the Windy Mountains, and it was definitely the sort of place dragons liked. But Adolphus was flummoxed by the lack of any obvious cave entrance.

"It was really big! Just here! I know it was . . ."

"Well, there's a bit of a crack in the rocks just here," said Olivia doubtfully, putting one claw into an extremely small gap between two sheer rock faces.

"You couldn't get flea in that, never mind a fully grown dragon," said Max. "We must have come the wrong way."

"No, no, no, no, no! It's here! I know it is!" insisted Adolphus, who started clambering up the rock face and putting his head into small crevices and sniffing around. "I know it's here . . . If I can just . . . Aaaaarrrrggghhh!"

His front claws slipped on the rock and his back legs scrabbled furiously. He tried to use his wings to help, but small stones and rocks were hurtling down the hillside around him and he started to slip. There was a grinding sound, and another yell, and then clouds of dust rose up in the air around him. When they settled, Adolphus had vanished. Where he'd been there was a small dark hole in the hillside.

Max peered into it. There was almost sheer rock plunging steadily downwards as far as he could see.

"Are you all right?" he called down the hole.

A very faint cry came from below, but it was impossible to tell if it was a cry for help or of triumph.

"Well, looks like we're in for another death-defying leap into the unknown," said Ferocious with resignation in his voice.

"We'll have to go down there," agreed Olivia. "Adolphus might be hurt. And besides, it must be the cave we were looking for. We need to get you another cauldron, Max."

Max peered down the dark hole again and then took a deep breath.

"Yes. Of course. Right then. Here we go."

He poked one back leg in, then another, then looked back at Ferocious and Olivia with a pained expression and let go. He hurtled downwards and plunged into the depths of the hill, mostly protected by his tough dragon scales but occasionally squealing as a sharp piece of rock dug into his flesh. The steep, rocky slope gradually levelled out as it reached the bottom, and finally Max was deposited, in a tangle of wings and claws and tail, on the sandy floor of a small cavern deep in the hillside. Almost immediately Olivia fell sprawling on top of him, and a second later Ferocious landed with a plop on the sand next to them both.

"Well, could have been worse," he observed, inspecting his coat and checking his tail carefully. "Seem to have most of my fur, at least."

The cavern they were in was small and very dimly lit by a glow coming from one corner. Max crept forward to investigate. There was a small opening in the rocky wall of the cavern, and beyond it another great chamber opened out in front of them. Here they could see clearly the source of the dim light.

A huge dragon lay in the centre of the cavern, surrounded by piles of shimmering gold and silver, all lit by strange glowing globes attached to the rocky walls. Adolphus was bouncing happily in front of the dragon, who was regarding him with one rather baleful eye.

"No, no, not 'A-doll's-house' . . . *Adolphus* . . .

Your great-nephew. I came to visit you before, remember? With Mum — er — Belissaria."

The dragon opened the other eye and rumbled deeply.

"Belissaria? Well, why didn't you say so? Instead of all this nonsense about doll's houses. Belissaria's boy. Well. Pleased to meet you!" She raised her great head and looked across the cavern at Max and Olivia.

"And these two young dragons are your friends, are they?"

Max and Olivia approached cautiously, lowering their heads in a kind of dragon bow. Adolphus's Great-Aunt Wilhelmina looked extremely large and forbidding, her great gleaming green body stretching out behind her into the depths of the cavern, and her head alone was twice the size of Adolphus. She looked at them for a moment and then sniffed.

"Hmm. Humans, I see. Long time since I've seen any humans in dragon form. Someone's got some powerful magic."

"That's Max," said Adolphus eagerly. "He's

brilliant. He turned everyone into frogs and then I kissed them and *whoosh!* they were dragons! He's really clever!"

The great dragon turned her head and looked hard at Max with her bright golden eyes. He coughed, and tried to return her gaze.

"It was . . . well . . . the frogspell was an accident, really, to start with, and then . . ." He trailed off into silence as her golden eyes continued to drill through him.

"Ah, yes . . . I see that you are a Pendragon," said Great-Aunt Wilhelmina at last, with satisfaction, and nodded her head slowly. "Well, that would explain it. Very good. I'm glad you've found a magical friend, A-dormouse."

"Adolphus," said the small dragon with exasperation. "A*dol*phus! And please — we were wondering — the reason we came — could Max have one of your cauldrons? His got a bit . . . um . . . battered, when I . . . er . . . fell in it."

Great-Aunt Wilhelmina drew herself up.

"One of my cauldrons? One of my *collection*?" she said, in an exceedingly shocked voice. "What an impertinence! I have *never* given a *single* cauldron to *anyone* before! They're MINE!" And her voice turned into a roar, and the roar turned into a gout of fire that lit the whole cavern with crackling blue-white flames.

Adolphus retreated rapidly, along with Max and Olivia.

"Er ... sorry ... sorry ... It was just ... well, it was my fault, and I thought ... er ... um ..."

Great-Aunt Wilhelmina looked down at them from the forbidding height she had raised herself to, and she appeared to soften slightly. She considered.

"Well, A-dog-nose. Maybe I might consider ... a small cauldron. But I require payment in return. A favour."

"Of course," said Max, quickly. "Anything we can do. Just ask."

The great dragon twisted her head, and looked at them with a calculating expression.

"A rockfall blocked my cave entrance a few years ago. I'm stuck here. I spent quite a few happy months rearranging my collection and composing my memoirs and such . . . but I've been getting rather bored. I'll give you a cauldron . . . if you can get me out of here."

There was silence while Max looked at all the others, and they looked back.

"Could you . . . make her smaller?" said Olivia at last.

Max made a face. "Maybe. If I had the spell ingredients. And a cauldron that worked. Neither of which are in my pack."

And then he yelled as Ferocious came up behind him, and nipped his ankle.

"Hey! What was that for?"

"For being as thick as a carrot," replied Ferocious. "Must be being a dragon. Affected your brain. What *have* you got in the pack, Max? Remind me again."

Max stared at him, and then his face brightened. "Of course! The frogspell! Well done, Ferocious!" He turned to Great-Aunt Wilhelmina.

"We can turn you into a frog. Or a rat, if you prefer — if Ferocious can transform you once you're a frog . . ."

The rat looked rather alarmed at the thought of kissing Great-Aunt Wilhelmina, even in frog form, but he swallowed hard, and nodded.

"Excellent!" said Max. "Well then, er . . . Lady Wilhelmina . . . Are you ready?"

He uncorked the blue frogspell bottle and, having considered the enormous size of the dragon, threw most of the contents at her head.

BANG!

The dragon disappeared and there, perched on the top of the huge pile of silver, gold and cauldrons, was a knobbly gold and green frog.

"Thank you," she croaked, "but I think on the whole a rat would be easier . . ." She looked at Ferocious expectantly. Closing his eyes, he planted a whiskery kiss on her head and there she was, in a haze of purple stars, a rather large and elderly rat, peering around at them all.

"Good," she said. "Well, then . . . I think I owe you a cauldron, Max."

She scampered off down the huge pile and started to poke around at the edges, further down into the cavern.

"Aha! This is the one!"

She rolled a small, dull-looking pewter cauldron out of the pile and looked up at Max.

"There you are. Not too ostentatious. Perfect for a young apprentice," she said, with an odd gleam in her eyes.

Max looked at all the wonderful silver and golden cauldrons, encrusted with jewels or decorated with fine carvings, piled on top of each other in the cavern, and then at the small, dull black one she was pointing at.

"Thank you," he said, trying hard not to sound too disappointed. He put it carefully in his pack, along with what was left of the frogspell, and slung the bag around his scaly neck. "I suppose we'd better head off, then."

Getting back up the steep slope was a lot harder than coming down, but eventually Max poked his dragon snout out of the hole into the open air and looked carefully around. There didn't seem to be anyone there. He eased himself out and then helped the others, one by one, as they squeezed out and fell on the rocky ground by the pool. None of them noticed the bushes on the other side of the pool rustling, or caught a glimpse of Snotty Hogsbottom's pale face peeping out from behind the crooked hawthorn tree, as they flopped down among the rocks to recover from the climb.

***

Great-Aunt Wilhelmina was overjoyed to be out in the fresh air after three years in the darkness of the cavern. Adolphus did his duty as a great-nephew and kissed her back to her dragon form, and she stretched her magnificent wings out and shook her great head happily.

"Well, well, A-doleful. So good of you to drop by with your friends . . . And thank you, Max, for getting me out of there. I really feel like a good holiday. Visit a few friends down south, maybe scout out a few new cauldrons for my collection. It should all be quite safe here in the mountain till I get back."

"Umm, how will you get back in?" asked Olivia, looking at the huge dragon, and the very small hole they'd just crawled out of.

Great-Aunt Wilhelmina laughed, a rumbling, fiery sort of laugh. "Oh, don't worry about that, little Pendragon!" she said. "From this side I've got a nice clear run at it. I can blast my way back into the cavern with a few good kicks." She flexed her great back legs, and Max scrambled back out of the way. She was undoubtedly right. In fact she could probably flatten the entire mountain with a few good kicks. He was glad she seemed to be relatively friendly.

"I suppose we'd better be getting back to the castle," he said. But at that moment, they heard a huge commotion further into the forest, and the crashing and neighing of horses, and then a great hunting horn, answered by another, and another, from all around.

They looked at each other, eyes wide.

"It's a hunt!" said Olivia.

"That's not a normal hunting horn," said Max.

"It's a dragon hunt!" said Adolphus, with a high-pitched squeal. "It's a wild dragon hunt! Help! Murder! Run! Fly!" He flapped his wings in panic, took off — and crashed straight into a low-hanging branch.

Max and Olivia felt equally terrified. It sounded as if the hunt was closing in — someone had realized there were dragons in this corner of the wood, and surrounded them. They were pinned against the mountain, and there was nowhere to go but up and out into the open, where they could be shot at with arrows. It didn't look good.

Ferocious scampered up Max's neck and bit his dragon ear. "Max!" he hissed. "Change back! Quickly!"

Of course! Max had the antidote in his pack! He slid it off his neck and reached for the antidote bottle. Rapidly he pulled the stopper off with his teeth and shook the bottle at Olivia and then over himself. Within seconds they were standing, looking slightly shaken, but definitely human. Now for Adolphus. Max grabbed the frogspell bottle, hurled a drop onto the still dazed Adolphus and watched in relief as he shrank to a rather knobbly blueish frog with green spots. He turned to Great-Aunt Wilhelmina, who'd been watching with interest, one ear twitching at the sound of the hunt coming nearer. She looked down her long dragon nose at him.

"No, thank you, young Pendragon. Once as a frog is quite enough. And I'm not the slightest bit worried by this little collection of horses and humans — when you've got to the ripe old age of four hundred and forty-three, you no longer have to fear such things as dragon hunts. Since it looks as if you and my great-nephew are quite safe, I think I'll be off." She stretched out her great wings, and raised her head up into the sky. The sound of horns and neighing suddenly redoubled, and she grinned and then looked back down at Max with her piercing golden eyes. "Something tells me I'll be seeing you again, Max . . . Farewell till then. And good luck with your spells!"

She took off, straight up into the sky. Suddenly the horns stopped, and Max could sense the entire hunt looking up in wonder at the huge dragon circling above them. She roared, and gouts of flame came scorching across the sky and burnt the tops of the tallest forest trees. The horses cried out in terror, and their riders were too busy trying to control them to even think about shooting at the dragon, who was almost immediately too high to reach anyway. With a last roar, she shot off into the sun and was gone.

"Max! Oliv—er!" came a familiar shout as the first of the horses rushed into the clearing where they were standing. "What on earth are you doing out here in the forest? Didn't you know there's a hunt on?"

"Um, no, sorry," said Max, as Sir Bertram swept up to them, looking extremely surprised. "We came out looking for — er — mushrooms, and then we sort of . . . got lost. Can you give us a ride back to the castle?"

Spying for Merlin

Sir Bertram told them off most of the way home for wandering around in the middle of a serious dragon hunt like a pair of idiots. When they finally got back to their room, Olivia turned Adolphus back to his usual dragon form, while Max unpacked his new cauldron. He had thanked Great-Aunt Wilhelmina politely when she gave it to him, but now he wondered if she'd really been that generous.

It was dull-looking with age, plain pewter with just a very simple decoration around the rim, which, now that he rubbed at it, looked like it might be pearls, but they were very small and worn ... And he wasn't entirely sure it was the right shape. It looked almost as lopsided as the one Adolphus had fallen into.

"Probably be even worse than the one I've got," he observed gloomily to Ferocious that evening.

But he was wrong. The new cauldron, plain and old as it was, turned out to be rather effective. From that point on, Max was indisputably top of the class. Every spell he made was perfect. He built a spell wall so strong even Aleric couldn't walk through it. He turned all the water in the moat pink, and then yellow, and then back to sludgy green, with a few sprinkles of colour-changing potion. He grew Aleric's beard down to his knees in a matter of seconds and then removed it all in an instant, to the acclaim of the entire class. But best of all was when they revisited the "lighter than air" spell and tried it on themselves this time. Max's potion was so strong the whole class ended up using a few drops of it, and they spent the afternoon bouncing off the ceiling, the walls and each other, cartwheeling happily around the roof like a bunch of apprentice-shaped balloons.

Meanwhile, Olivia had finally had a showdown with Mordred, and managed to punch him so hard in the nose that he had to spend the rest of the day with a poultice attached to his face to stop the swelling — to the general amusement of the other squires. After that, he avoided Olivia, and she found herself thoroughly enjoying the training. She beat all of them at Find Your Way Through the Slimy Swamp Maze (mostly because she was smallest and lightest), and she also managed to gain the class honours for hitting the archery target right in the bullseye three times in a row.

By the end of the week, both Max and Olivia were Most Improved Student of the Week, and Sir Bertram had taken to walking around the castle with a slight swagger, twirling his huge moustache, and telling anyone who would listen about his son's and his, *er, hmm,* nephew's successes.

It was Ferocious, as usual, who brought them back to earth.

"Impressed as I am by your excellent progress in your lessons . . . you do realize that we have been here two weeks already and we haven't got the faintest idea what Morgana's up to?"

They were lounging around in their room, and Max and Olivia had been swapping stories about just how brilliant they were. At Ferocious's words, they both looked slightly put out, but then Max nodded.

"You're right. We haven't even tried . . . And it's much more important than lessons, really . . ." He fingered the swift that had been sitting all this time in his belt pouch and thought of Merlin. He felt hot all over realizing that he'd not even tried to do any spying on Morgana. He thought of her pale, icy face and those hard blue eyes and shivered. Was it because he was too scared of her? But Merlin was relying on him. He couldn't let him down.

Max took a deep breath.

"All right. We need to make an effort to get close to her. Any plotting is going to happen in secret, in her chambers. Any ideas?"

"Well, it would probably make sense not to be human," said Olivia. "Can we turn ourselves into ants or earwigs or something?"

"Um, not really," said Max. "I don't think we're going to be able to find an insect willing to kiss a couple of frogs."

"Rats," said Olivia.

"Yes, I know it's annoying, but we could think of something else," replied Max.

"No, stupid! I meant, we can *be* rats," she said. "Ferocious will kiss us. Oh — and Max! — I've just remembered! I saw Caradoc the other day and he told me he's been invited to sing in Lady Morgana's chambers this evening. Private party. He was ever so excited; it's a real honour for him. Do you think, if it's a private gathering, there might be something fishy going on?"

"Probably a gathering of the Castle Ladies' Weaving Circle," said Ferocious. "But you never know. At least we'd be doing something. And I have to say, from my explorations so far, the walls of this castle have got more holes in them than a piece of your mother's knitting. We can go anywhere we want, not even lose a whisker."

"Excellent," said Max, happily. "Then we're set. Frogs to rats to intrepid spies. Transformation coming right up!"

***

The private chambers of Lady Morgana le Fay were dark and luxurious, hung around with velvet and lit by glowing candles and deep red firelight. The lady herself was draped elegantly across an ornately carved and richly upholstered bench seat, and looked completely at home. Sir Richard Hogsbottom, perched next to her on a low footstool, looked less relaxed. The heat was making him sweat slightly, and his ample frame was balanced uncomfortably on the stool like a large toad sitting on a pointy mushroom. Across from them, Snotty was standing with his back to the fire, looking quite at ease. His pale face was totally focused on the fourth figure in the room, Caradoc the Bard.

Caradoc was leaning forward on a low seat, tracing shapes on the floor of the chamber, shapes that glimmered slightly silver before fading away as he drew new ones. He seemed to be in the middle of explaining something, and the others were all watching him intently.

"The song is not always clear," he said, gesturing to the shapes in front of him. "But there are seven challenges, and they must all be overcome. The Fortress of Grog Insobriety," — and as he spoke he swirled another silvery shape on the floor — "the Flaming Door, the Nine Maidens," — the silvery trail took nine dancing shapes — "the Stream of Jet, the Fortress of Glass, protected by a silent sentinel, the Brindled Ox, and the Hounds of Annwn. Seven only can return — and only if they have payment."

He drew his hand across in front of him and the silvery shapes disappeared.

"Payment," said Morgana with a smile. "Oh yes, they will have the necessary payment." She laughed, a sharp sliver of laughter that cut through the warmth of the room like a blade.

"The Treasure of Annwn," said Caradoc softly, and he looked up at Morgana with a strange expression. "You mean . . . you have it?"

She smiled sweetly. "I believe it is in our possession. Is it not, Adrian?"

"Yes, my lady. I've found it."

"Ah," put in Sir Richard, not wanting to be left out. "But we're not sure which one it is, eh? Are we, Adrian?"

Snotty looked annoyed, but continued confidently. "Not *exactly* sure. But I'm working on it. A bit of . . . sorting . . . to do, before we find the exact one."

Morgana gave him a hard stare, but he returned it without flinching. She nodded, satisfied.

"So," she said. "We are prepared. Arthur will take the bait; it is just the sort of idiotically chivalrous quest he specializes in. And then he will be lost, by his own actions, and we shall be seen to have had no part in it. He is doomed, and we shall get rid of that fool Merlin at the same time. And then I — I shall be Queen!" And she raised her white arms and smiled in triumph and her expression was quite terrible.

Snotty gave a small, secret smile. But Sir Richard eased his finger around the collar of his tunic and swallowed. He really couldn't get used to all this talk of getting rid of people. He was all for Lady Morgana being Queen, of course, and rather fancied himself as her trusty second-in-command. But he did wish it could be done without actually . . . well . . . killing anyone. His eye was caught by a gleam in the wall next to him. Was that a rat, poking its nose out of the wall? He leant forward to peer more closely . . . but the beast had vanished. Trick of the light, most likely, he thought. Trick of the light.

"Well!" said Olivia, when they were all back in their room. "That stinking, rotten, slimy two-faced traitorous rat, Caradoc!"

"Er — hmm," said Ferocious. "That stinking rotten slimy two-faced traitorous *human*, Caradoc, I think you'll find."

Max was rubbing his leg where it had gone numb, and yawning. They'd been squashed inside the walls of Lady Morgana's chambers for hours, waiting for the private party to end and the various knights and ladies to retire. Only at midnight, when most of them had gone, had the secret discussions started.

"I thought he was a friend!" went on Olivia. "I shared a horse with him! He kissed me! Urghh! And all the time he was coming here to help Morgana."

Max shook his head, trying to get the sleepiness out of it. There was something about the scene they'd just witnessed that bothered him. Something they weren't getting, something he needed to remember. But he was just too tired to think.

"We need to go to bed," he said at last. "We'll decide what to do in the morning."

***

The next morning they gathered, still yawning, in the castle stables. Olivia was on mucking-out duty and Max had the day off.

"So, what are we going to do?" said Olivia, forking bundles of mucky straw into the stable yard. "Should we send that swift to Merlin, do you think?"

Max was leaning against one of the stable partitions, trying to keep out of the way of flying horse manure. Adolphus was scampering around, pouncing on insects who'd just lost their cozy hideaway.

"I don't know," said Max. "I don't think we know enough yet."

"We know Caradoc's a dirty, stinking, rotten—"

"Yes, yes, I know, that's one thing. But we have no idea what the plot actually is. And there's something funny about it all."

Max closed his eyes and put his finger in his ear. Sometimes it helped him think. Olivia stopped forking straw and watched him. After a few minutes, he opened his eyes and frowned.

"They said Arthur would take the bait — it was a chivalrous quest or some such. And then there was all that stuff Caradoc was spouting about . . . about the Nine Maidens and the Brindled Ox and what have you. And the Hounds of Annwn."

"Yes, what was all that about?"

"I'm not sure," said Max. "But Annwn is the place where magic comes from. It's a kind of Otherworld, supposed to be full of strange magic creatures, tricks and amazing food and drink and music . . ."

"Doesn't sound too dangerous."

"But I don't think they let humans go there, generally. And I'm pretty sure if they go there they never come back."

"But Caradoc said something about coming back — he said you could come back, if you had payment. That was when they started talking about the Treasure of Annwn. It's what Snotty was supposed to have found."

"Yes," said Max. "And that's it! That's the bit that's been bothering me. He said that to get back from this quest, Arthur would need the Treasure of Annwn as payment. But they don't want Arthur to get back. So why are they bothering to look for this treasure?"

Ferocious, who'd been burrowing about in the straw for a few bits of breakfast, jumped up onto the edge of the drinking trough and nodded. "It's a good point. You're definitely improving, Max. The king needs the treasure to get back. But they don't want him to get back. So Snotty's busy looking for the treasure. Doesn't make any sense to me, either."

Olivia shrugged. "Maybe they need it for some other reason. Maybe it's worth loads of money."

"I don't know," said Max. "But I know we need to find out. We've got two more weeks before Merlin and Arthur get here. We need to start doing some serious spying. We need to be in the castle walls, listening out for anything we can."

The Treasure of Annwn

For the rest of that week, Max and Olivia spent every minute they could spare from lessons as rats, sneaking around the castle walls. Meanwhile, Ferocious spent every minute they were in lessons as himself, also sneaking around the castle walls. Between them they discovered any number of secrets. Secrets about who was in love with Lady Marianne the Fair (everyone between the ages of fifteen and fifty), secrets about how the castle cook got the mutton to taste so good (boiling it with dried toad skin) and secrets about how Sir Uriel always managed to win at card games (he had an enchanted cheating pack). But none of these secrets got them anywhere near finding out what Lady Morgana was up to.

By the end of the week they were falling asleep in lessons and thoroughly fed up with crawling through small cracks in the castle walls, discovering nothing. Even worse, the frogspell bottle was looking distinctly empty. There was probably only enough for one or two more transformations before Max would have to try and steal enough ingredients from the castle spell store to make some more.

"I ache all over," complained Olivia, stretching out on the grass by the moat. It was a thoroughly hot day, the sun reflecting off the castle walls and the air shimmering. The squires and apprentices had been given the afternoon off, and most of them were splashing around in the moat, but Max and Olivia were too tired even to swim. They were sprawled on the grass with Adolphus laid out next to them, basking in the sun like a lizard.

Max was chewing a piece of grass and looking thoughtful.

"There's something wrong with what we're doing," he said. "We've spent ages sneaking around, but we haven't really found out anything."

"I know," groaned Olivia. "If I hear one more person profess undying love to Lady Marianne, I'm going to be sick."

"I don't think the interesting stuff is happening in the castle at all at the moment — maybe they're up to something somewhere else. Snotty is out every day — he leaves early in the morning and doesn't get back till late at night. What's he up to?"

"Well, perhaps if someone followed him, we might find out," suggested Ferocious.

"But we'll miss lessons," objected Olivia. "And I really need to be there tomorrow. We're practising disarming manoeuvres and I've beaten everyone so far, except Eric. If I beat him tomorrow, I'll be Squire of the Week."

Max looked at her and raised his eyebrows. "Oh, well then, of course you'd better stay. I'll just have to miss learning how to make a swamp solid instead. And when I'm sucked down to a muddy death in the Great Grimpen Mire, I'm sure it'll be a great comfort to me that you were once Squire of the Week."

"Oh, stop griping!" said Ferocious. "You can both go to your ever-so-important lessons. Adolphus and I will do it."

"Oh, yes please!" said Adolphus, lifting his head eagerly. "I'll sneak after Snotty! Very, very quietly. I know I can do it!"

Max looked doubtful — but he did really want to go to tomorrow's lesson. It was the last one with Aleric. The following day they started a week with Lady Morgana herself, and that was not going to be half as much fun.

"Okay," he said at last. "Ferocious, you're in

charge. And make sure he doesn't see you."

Ferocious rolled his eyes. "Of course," he said scornfully. "He won't suspect a thing."

***

Snotty Hogsbottom was in an extremely bad mood. He and Jerome had spent nearly a week searching the dragon's hoard — pulling out bits of treasure, stacking piles of cauldrons, rearranging gold and silver and precious ornaments — and he still hadn't found what he was looking for. Worse, today they had been ordered to take Caradoc the Bard along with them to help. Snotty was not happy about having anyone else there to share the glory if they found the Treasure of Annwn. Jerome didn't count, but Caradoc had already wormed his way into Morgana's good books with his knowledge of ancient lore and his silvery spells. Snotty would happily have turned him into a snail if he'd known how.

At the cavern entrance, Snotty grumpily indicated the ropes they had put in place to help with the climb down.

"After you," he said, with exaggerated politeness, and Caradoc nodded and lowered himself carefully down. Snotty considered cutting the rope with his hunting knife, but then shrugged and headed down after him. Morgana would have words to say if he came back without the bard, and Morgana's words generally had the effect of leaving you upside down in a pile of steaming horse manure.

When they reached the dragon's cavern, Caradoc stopped, and whistled.

"No wonder it's taken a week," he said, surveying the vast pile of gold and a slightly smaller pile of other stuff that had been sorted and stacked. "How many cauldrons did she have?"

"We're not sure," said Jerome with an apologetic glance at Snotty, who had stalked off to start pulling things out of the remaining pile. "It's rumoured as many as two thousand."

"My word," said Caradoc in admiration. "What an obsession! Makes our job difficult, eh?"

By mid-afternoon, Snotty was feeling more well-disposed toward Caradoc. He was a willing worker and had pulled out, sorted and discarded at least fifty cauldrons. Best of all, none of them had been the Treasure of Annwn. Not that Snotty had found it either, but at least Caradoc hadn't beaten him to it.

It was while they were resting, backs against the huge pile of as-yet unsorted gold, chewing bread and cold meat, that Snotty thought he heard something.

He held his hand up for silence and they all listened. There was definitely a flapping sound high in the roof of the cavern. And a squeaking. They hardly had time to exchange glances, before the squeaking rose to a crescendo, and hundreds of bats suddenly dived from the roof and started swirling around the cavern like a writhing mass of black smoke. In their midst, looking rather disoriented, was a small blue-green dragon, flapping its wings to try to drive the bats away and looking like it might crash into the cavern wall at any minute. Which, after a few more bats had flown into its ears, was exactly what it did. It hit the rocky wall with a thump and slid down to the sandy floor, dazed and confused.

Snotty was on his feet in an instant and had the dragon by the throat.

"Right! Got you, you stupid dozy interfering beast," he snarled. "Max sent you spying, eh? Didn't he know better than to send such a brainless waste of space? Well, now you've had it, dragon. Now you're dead meat."

***

The sun was setting to the west of Castle Gore, and shadows were stretching out across the courtyard. Max and Olivia were taking turns to peer anxiously out of the narrow arched window of their room, hoping to catch a flash of blue-green flying over the castle walls, but so far they'd seen nothing.

"Do you think they're all right?" asked Olivia, again. She was frantic with worry about Adolphus, and she would have given her newly acquired Squire of the Week certificate ten times over just for news that he was safe.

Max was trying not to show it, but he was equally worried. Adolphus and Ferocious should have been back ages ago. Most of the castle had retired to their chambers, and they had seen Snotty return hours before. As he took his turn at the window, Max fingered the swift, still in his belt pouch, and wondered if he should have sent it off when they first heard of Morgana's plans. He had wanted to have more to tell, to have learnt the whole plot, to have earned Merlin's admiration and gratitude. And now Adolphus and Ferocious were in trouble, and it was all his fault. He nearly groaned — and then he suddenly sat up straight, widened his eyes and shouted in glee.

"They're back! Olivia — they're back! There they are!"

Adolphus came swooping in over the battlements, straight toward the window, and Max only just got out of the way before he hurtled through it and came to a skittering halt in the middle of the floor, panting.

"Is it gone? Is it gone? Did we get away?"

Ferocious dropped off his neck and said soothingly, "It's okay, Adolphus, you managed to leave the nasty scary owl behind ages ago! We're safe."

Adolphus breathed a mighty sigh of relief and flopped down sideways with his eyes rolled up into his head and his tongue stuck out. Olivia threw herself at him and hauled him onto her lap, stroking his scaly back and tickling him under his chin.

"Adolphus, I'm so glad you're back. We were really worried!"

Ferocious had leapt up onto Max's shoulder and was nibbling his ear affectionately.

"Well, yes, you should have been. He was very nearly put in a pie. If it hadn't been for Caradoc, he would have been."

"Caradoc?" said Olivia with distaste. "That traitor?"

"Yes. He might be working for Morgana, but he's still a friend of dragons," said Ferocious. "We

122

followed Snotty and Caradoc to Great-Aunt Wilhelmina's cavern, but then we got caught. Snotty was all for chopping Adolphus into little bite-sized morsels but Caradoc wouldn't hear of it. Bad luck to eat dragons, he said. So they just left us in the cave and rolled a stone across the entrance."

"Then how did you get out?" asked Max.

"Well, that's the thing," said Ferocious, puzzled. "About an hour ago, someone came and rolled the stone away again. We heard them shift it, but when we got up there, we couldn't see a thing. So we just headed back to the castle. And here we are. And we've discovered something."

Ferocious paused for effect as Olivia and Max both looked at him, expectantly.

"It's a cauldron," he said, at last, meaningfully.

"What?"

"The Treasure of Annwn," said the rat, looking around at them all. "It's part of Great-Aunt Wilhelmina's hoard. It's a cauldron."

There was silence as they all digested this. Then

Olivia looked up at Max, open-mouthed.

"But Max . . ."

"Yes," said Ferocious. "I think it's definitely possible."

Max shook his head. "*My* cauldron? The one she gave me? But she wouldn't have given me a really precious one! Anyway, it doesn't look like anything special. It's really old and dull."

"But it's very magical," observed Ferocious. "Or were you just thinking it was you, Max? Getting so much better at this spell business?"

Max frowned. It was true his spells had been spectacularly better since he'd got the new cauldron — but then the old one had been so totally ruined by Adolphus, that just having a decent, working cauldron could have helped. He shook his head.

"No, I'm sure it's just ordinary. Maybe a bit better than your average apprentice's cauldron — but I'm sure it can't be the one they're looking for."

"But Max," said Olivia, "you've got lessons with Morgana tomorrow. Don't you think you'd better take your old one, in case? Until we find out more?"

Max looked stubborn. He really didn't want to make an idiot of himself in front of Morgana le Fay. He couldn't face another disaster like the ones in his first week. Besides, Great-Aunt Wilhelmina had had thousands of cauldrons, and she'd known exactly where each one had come from. She'd never have given him such an important one.

"No," he said firmly. "I'm taking that one. It's just an old cauldron from some wizard or other she met on her travels. It'll be fine."

Spells and Cauldrons

The next morning, Olivia left Max snoring and crept out clutching the bottle of frogspell, with Ferocious on her shoulder. Max, having had one scare already, had expressly forbidden any further spying till he had contacted Merlin — but Olivia couldn't resist. Morgana le Fay would be teaching at the Spell School all morning — so she wouldn't be in her chambers. What better time to search them and see if there were any clues about what she was up to? Ferocious had already promised to keep Max company for his lessons, so it was up to her. She rapidly turned herself into a frog, and Ferocious, wrinkling up his nose, gave her a whiskery rat kiss before scampering back to Max with the potion bottle.

Now, after crawling her way slowly through to Morgana's part of the castle, Olivia was beginning to wish she'd listened to Max and just gone off to squire lessons as usual. The walls of Morgana's chambers had an odd, spicy smell that Olivia remembered from the last time she had been there. It made her rat nose tickle and her eyes water. She tried to find the gap they'd peeped through last time, but the walls were a maze of little crooked spaces between stones and it was hard to work out where she was. She seemed to have reached a dead end and, as she tried to turn around, whacked her head painfully on a protruding bit of stone. Trolls' toenails! Maybe this had not been such a good idea after all.

Suddenly there was a crash. Olivia stiffened. There was a long silence, and then the sound of someone moving around furtively in the room beyond. Olivia crept forward, using the sounds to guide her, until she was peering between two stones directly into Morgana's chamber. The morning light streamed in through the tall arched windows and dust motes whirled in the sunbeams. Dust motes that were being scattered and disturbed by a tall figure striding through the room, upturning objects and pulling back velvet draperies, quietly and methodically searching every corner. It was Caradoc.

Olivia drew in a breath. What was he doing here? Had Morgana sent him to get something? But then why was he searching so thoroughly — surely she'd have told him where to look? Was he here in secret? He started to look carefully at a large cupboard on the other side of the room. Her rat nose twitched as she poked it out of the gap in the stones. She couldn't see what he was doing, but if she jumped down, she could hide behind a tapestry and watch him more closely.

Olivia took a deep breath and jumped. As she emerged from the wall, there was a loud *pop!* and she landed sprawled on the floor, arms and legs flailing, completely human.

Caradoc turned around instantly and had his hand over her mouth before she even had time to yell. She struggled, trying to tell him he was a lousy, rotten slimeball, but his grip was firm. He leant his face close to hers and whispered urgently, "Not a sound, Olivia, if you value your life!"

She stopped struggling and looked at him, wide-eyed. How did he know her name? Or that she was really a girl? What was going on?

Caradoc released his grip slightly and then, when she made no sound, nodded.

"Good. Now perhaps you'd better tell me what you're doing here."

Olivia looked at him angrily. "I'm not telling you anything. You're working for that evil witch. And when Merlin gets here I hope he turns you into a dung beetle!"

Caradoc laughed and clapped Olivia on the back. "Well said! But I'm not working for Morgana, I'm working for Merlin."

"Merlin!" said Olivia in surprise. "But — we saw you, you were here, in her chambers, plotting!"

Caradoc frowned. "So you heard that, did you? Well, yes, I was here, apparently plotting. I have been doing my best to win my Lady Morgana's trust. But I am still in the outer circle. I am still a long way from knowing the whole plot. Which is why I am here, just now, while she is away."

"Me, too," said Olivia. "But how come I got changed back into a girl? I was a rat, in the walls . . ."

"Ah, well, the chamber is enchanted," said Caradoc. "It strips away all magic spells from those who enter. It did the same to me." He smiled ruefully. "I'd used some potion Merlin gave me to become a sparrow. You probably heard the noise as I was changed back and fell off the window ledge."

Olivia grinned. "So that was what that crash was. Well, I suppose it's easier to search her room with hands rather than wings. Have you found anything?"

Caradoc shook his head. "No. But I think if there is anything, it will be in this cupboard here. It has a peculiar lockspell on it, I was trying to disentangle it when you arrived." He moved toward the cupboard, which was tall and narrow, with dark, carved oak doors.

"Are you a wizard, then, as well as a bard?" asked Olivia.

Caradoc laughed. "Oh, a little bit of a wizard, and a little bit of a bard. And — a little bit of a knight," he said, and touched his finger to the side of his long crooked nose. "But mostly whatever Merlin wants me to be, whatever is most useful. My true name is not Caradoc. But — perhaps that had better stay my name for now. Caradoc the Bard, as always, at your service, my lady," and he swept her an elaborate bow.

Olivia made a face. "I'm not a lady. I'm a squire. And I'm going to be a knight, too."

"So you are," said Caradoc, gravely. "I had forgotten."

He turned back to the cupboard, and passed his hands across the front with a strange flourish. "There. It's undone. Now, let's have a look, shall we?"

He carefully opened both tall narrow doors and they peered inside. There were several shelves, all crammed with pots and potion bottles and flasks in every colour of glass, so that it looked like a cupboard full of jewels. In the middle were three small drawers, and Caradoc, after a glance at the potion bottles, pulled the drawers out one after the other. They were filled with rolls of creamy parchment, tied with ribbons and attached to small packets of brightly coloured powders. One was loose, placed carelessly on the top of the pile as if it had been discarded there only recently. Olivia and Caradoc exchanged glances, and he pulled open the parchment and started to read.

"Well, well — a replica spell ... A cunning thing indeed. So that is how they will do it," he muttered. "This might come in useful." He pulled a piece of parchment and a quill out of what seemed like thin air and started to copy down the spell. He also took a few grains of the powder and carefully placed them in a twist of paper. Then he rolled up the original, put it back in the cupboard and again passed his hands across the front, remaking the lockspell. He stood for a few seconds, thinking, and then shook his head and turned to Olivia.

"We need to go. The Spell School will finish soon, and it wouldn't do to be found anywhere near these rooms. But I think we need to talk, you and Max and I. We definitely need to talk."

***

Caradoc was right — the Spell School was just about to finish. By the time they got down to Max and Olivia's room, there was only time for Olivia to dig out some oatcakes and a bottle of spiced apple juice, and put them on a small table, before Max burst into the room looking cross.

"What's *he* doing here?" he asked, when he saw Caradoc sitting, happily munching an oatcake. "Who invited *him*?"

"I did," said Olivia firmly — and pulled up another chair for Max. "Sit down. We need to talk. Caradoc's on our side — he's working for Merlin."

"Merlin?" said Max, falling into the chair and looking extremely surprised. "What? But how?"

Ferocious poked his nose out of Max's tunic and looked at Caradoc. "Ah, then, last to know anything, as usual. Glad it's Max, as well, and not just me this time. I suppose it must have been you who rolled the stone away from the cave last night, then?"

"Er, yes, it was," admitted Caradoc sheepishly. "Sorry you had to wait such a long time. I had to go back there after I'd returned to the castle with Adrian Hogsbottom."

"Snotty," said Max, automatically.

"Sorry?" said Caradoc.

"No — Snotty," said Olivia. "It's his name. Adrian's name. It's really Snotty."

"I see," said Caradoc. "Yes, I can see that it would be. Excellent. I won't make that mistake again." He grinned. "So, how much do you both know?"

"First," said Olivia. "We need to ask you — what does this Cauldron of Annwn look like? Because Great-Aunt Wilhelmina — that's the big dragon — she gave one to Max."

Caradoc's eyes widened; he sat up very straight.

"She gave Max a cauldron? *Gave* it to him?"

"Yes," said Max. "In exchange for us turning her small so she could get out of the cave."

Caradoc looked very excited. "Then — it might be — I can't believe it! Max, is it small and black, with a row of pearls around the edge?"

Max and Olivia looked at each other, and Olivia groaned.

"It is! It is the one! But Max took it to the Spell School today. Morgana must have seen it — and she's bound to have recognized it!"

"Is this true?" said Caradoc urgently. "Did she see it?"

Max paused, as they both looked at him anxiously, and then grinned.

"No. She didn't see it. Because I didn't take it.

Adolphus was asleep with his head inside it, and I didn't have the heart to wake him up. So I took the old one and instead of turning water into ink I turned it into jam. So I got a D. Which is why I was cross. But the cauldron is over there — by the fireplace."

They turned to look — and there it was, battered, dull and entirely ordinary looking, lying on its side with Adolphus's long blue-green body spilling out of it and the sound of dragon snores coming from inside. As they looked, there was a snuffle, and then a cough and then a sleepy-eyed Adolphus poked his head out and said:

"Hello! Is it morning?"

They heaved Adolphus out of the way, and Caradoc knelt down and examined the cauldron, turning it this way and that and squinting at the faded pearls.

"Yes," he said at last. "It's definitely the right one. What an amazing piece of luck. Or maybe — I don't know. They're wily creatures, old dragons. Maybe she had an inkling . . ." He looked hard at

Max and then smiled. "Whatever the reason, here it is. And now — we can get to work."

He took out the spell he'd copied from Morgana and waved it in front of them.

"A replica spell. It can make an exact copy of any object you have in front of you. That's why they need the cauldron. Not to give it to Arthur, but to make a copy — so Arthur will go to Annwn on his chivalrous quest, *thinking* he has the treasure and that he'll be able to use it as payment to return."

"But how are they planning to make him go to Annwn in the first place?" said Max.

"I don't know," said Caradoc. "Some scheme or other. Now we know, it shouldn't be too hard for him to find a way out of it. But if we can make them think they are safe, if we can make them think their plans are going perfectly — then maybe they will overstretch themselves. Maybe Lady Morgana will finally show Arthur her true face. Maybe we can catch them red-handed . . . And for that, we need them to think they have the real cauldron."

He unfolded the twist of paper he had taken from Morgana's room and scattered some grains of powder over the cauldron as he started to mutter the words of the spell. Then he took hold of the sides of the cauldron and started to pull his hands away, chanting as he did so. Before long, Max and Olivia could see a second cauldron, identical to the first, slowly forming in his hands; it was as if he were pulling a second copy out of the original, more and more of it emerging, until with a faint *pop!* the two separated — and there they were: two dusty, black, worn-looking cauldrons, each with a faint rim of pearls at the edge.

"Er — which one is the real one?" said Max, looking from one to the other.

"Hard to tell," said Caradoc, with a gleam in his eye. "Which do you think?"

Max looked from one to the other, and then grasped hold of them both. They looked identical, and they almost felt exactly the same, too — but when you held them at the same time, there was just the faintest hint of coldness from one, the slightest buzz of hidden magics from the other.

"This one," said Max, tapping it.

"Is indeed the Cauldron of Annwn," said Caradoc approvingly. "You have quite a gift for magic, Max — many full wizards could not tell the difference, even with the cauldrons right next to each other."

Max went slightly pink and tried not to look too pleased, while Olivia rolled her eyes.

"Yes, well, Max, we all know you're a genius. Try not to let your head swell too much or you won't be able to fit through the castle gatehouse."

Caradoc laughed. He picked up the false cauldron, wrapped it in his cloak, and started to head out of the door.

"How are you going to get it to Morgana?" asked Max.

"Oh, I think we'll let ... ah ... Snotty *discover* it at the dragon's hoard, shall we?" he said.

***

139

Max sat by the fire that evening, the creamy parchment of Merlin's swift spread out in front of him, a quill in his hand. They'd agreed he would let Merlin know all they had found out so far: that there was a plot to get Arthur to go on a quest to Annwn with a false cauldron so he would be unable to return; that he, Max, had the real cauldron and that Caradoc would be making sure Morgana got the copy. He wished he had more detail to give Merlin, but it would have to do; he said the words of the spell, released the swift, and it soared out of the window and into the night.

Despite Caradoc's certainty, Max still couldn't quite believe that his cauldron was the Treasure of Annwn, that it came from the Otherworld. He looked at it and sighed. He wouldn't be able to use it for the rest of the Spell School, anyway, and that meant struggling on with his old one. Caradoc had done some magical repairs, and it was looking a little less lopsided, but Max didn't hold out much hope.

He was going to fail the Spell School for sure.

Morgana's Magic

Max's lessons the next day were interrupted by the sudden appearance of Snotty Hogsbottom, looking like he'd just discovered a magic cauldron in a pile of dragon's gold. Max smiled to himself as he stirred his sparkling blue potion (Caradoc's repair spells seemed to be holding up). He watched Snotty's dark head bending over close to Morgana's own, and saw the look of triumph that flitted across her face. She looked up at the class and waved for silence.

"I'm afraid some *pressing* business has come up, so, sadly, I will have to leave you for the rest of the day," she announced sweetly. "I shall send for Aleric to take over. Keep stirring, and — Max — do try to make sure your potion is a *little* more accurate this time ..."

She gave him an icy smile, and Max looked back stonily. Then, with a dismissive wave of her hand, she swept out, with Snotty, looking smug, following behind.

Max went back to stirring, wondering what they would be doing. Making a copy of the copy, he supposed. Caradoc had told him that the spell could be used again and again, but that none of the copies would have the magic of the original, only its external appearance. Max was glad about that. Morgana's spells were strong enough without any extra help from a powerful Otherworld cauldron. He ground a few more grains of dried woodlouse spit and added them to the spell, watching for the characteristic red colour that would tell him it was working. He noticed Aleric enter the room and wondered if he'd take over for the rest of the Spell School while Morgana put her plans in place. There were still five more days before Arthur was due to arrive. Plenty of time for her to set her trap — but plenty of time, too, for them to find out what it was, and hopefully get enough evidence to prove to Arthur once and for all that she was an evil, scheming witch.

Max's potion turned bright red, and he grinned. Things were looking up. They were definitely looking up.

But Max didn't have much time to gloat. As they all transferred their potions to waiting bottles, Aleric came up and tapped him on the shoulder.

"Ah, Max. Lady Morgana expressly asked that you show her your potion when the class was over. She said you made such a mess of it yesterday that she wanted to be quite sure you'd got it right this time. I must say, I'm surprised. You were doing splendidly last week."

Max frowned. He was pretty sure his potion had gone fine today, but he really didn't want to have to put it to the test under Morgana's icy glare. Still — he brightened — maybe he'd get a chance to see or hear something useful.

"Okay," he said, packing up carefully. "Where should I take it?"

"She said she'd be down in the wine cellar, sorting out something to do with King Arthur's visit."

Better and better, thought Max. I really might get a chance to find something out. But Ferocious wasn't happy.

"Are you sure this is a good idea, Max? Going to meet Morgana le Fay in a dark part of the castle where no one can hear you scream?"

Max rolled his eyes. "She won't do anything, Ferocious. She's got King Arthur to worry about. She's not going to bother with me just when they've got the cauldron and their plans are all working out."

But Ferocious had a funny feeling about the whole thing. Just as Max reached the cellar door, the rat jumped down out of his belt pouch and slipped behind an old wine barrel. And it was just as well he did. Because the moment Max got through the door, he was hit by a sprinkling of Snotty's special immobility spell, and he toppled face first onto the hard cellar floor while his cauldron, bags and books went flying.

***

Max had always thought that Morgana le Fay was an extremely scary witch. Watching her now, silhouetted against flickering spell light, her arms wide and crackling with magic, her pale face focused on the cauldron in front of her, he realized that he had never fully understood how powerful she was. Max was strapped to a chair in the middle of the cellar. He had been tied up by Snotty, who had then removed the immobility spell and laughed nastily as Max tried to struggle out of his bonds.

"Don't bother, Pendragon. The more you pull, the tighter they'll get."

Morgana had now brought her cauldron up to

the perfect temperature and was adding the last-minute ingredients to her spell. As she scattered some silvery dust into the bubbling mixture, she turned to Max with a honey-sweet smile.

"My dear Max — so *good* of you, so *obliging* of you to come and show your potion to me. *Pity* it got spilled when you dived so enthusiastically to the floor, but never mind . . . You won't be needing it where you're going."

Max tried to look as nonchalant as possible, but he couldn't help wondering what she meant. Where was he going?

"We thought you'd like to take a little trip, Adrian and I," she explained. "We felt it would be a nice little *reward* for interfering in our plans in Camelot. And it suits us perfectly, because we're rather hoping a certain person will feel obliged to *rescue* you." She laughed, and her laughter was like glass shattering on the stone floor.

Max's heart sank. All the spying they'd done, all the bits of the plot they'd found out, and they'd completely missed the really important bit. The trap that would send Arthur to the land of Annwn. It was him! He was the bait! They were going to send him to Annwn and then King Arthur would *have* to rescue him. Max was so cross with himself for being such an idiot, that he didn't have any spare energy for being scared. If only he'd listened to Ferocious. If only he'd *thought* before trotting down to the cellar, hoping he might find out something important. He'd found out the rest of the plot, all right, but it wasn't going to do him much good, trussed up like a chicken and about to be magicked to the Otherworld.

Morgana lifted up her arms and started to chant the spell. Locks of her hair flared around her face and writhed like snakes. Her eyes were icy blue, so cold that Max felt himself freeze under their glance. Her face was pale and terrible. She stretched out her arms toward Max and called out in a harsh voice as she threw a sparkling drop of spell at him. Time seemed to slow down as Max watched the droplet arc across the space between them. But then there was a sudden commotion, the door slammed open, and a figure threw herself into the room and straight at Max. It was Olivia, and he barely had time to register her terrified face before the droplet landed on her outstretched hand and she disappeared like a light winking out.

***

Max woke up, feeling like he'd been drowned and then dragged out of the ocean depths by the scruff of his neck. His head felt fuzzy and everything hurt. The room he was in seemed strangely dim, and he couldn't quite focus on the person who seemed to be talking to him. He shook his head and tried to speak, but all that came out was a whisper.

"Ah, awake now?" said the voice, and Max thought he recognized it, but he wasn't sure. A hand waved across his face, and suddenly the room seemed brighter and his head hurt less. He realized he was in his own bed, and sitting nearby was . . .

"Merlin! What? You aren't supposed to be here yet! What's happened?"

Merlin looked down at him and patted his shoulder.

"I got your swift," he said. "It made me think that perhaps I should be here. But I wish I had arrived earlier." For some reason he was looking very gentle and sympathetic. "Max," he said, "can you remember anything?"

Max tried hard — but the last thing he remembered was the lesson . . . and then taking his potion down to the cellar . . .

"I was on my way to the wine cellar — to see Lady Morgana," he said, slowly. "Then — I don't remember . . ."

"You have had your memory spelled away," said Merlin. And then, choosing his words with care, "It seems that the same enchantress who stole away the Cornish prince has returned. She tricked Aleric into thinking she was Lady Morgana and tried to send you to the land of Annwn. Instead, she succeeded in sending Olivia."

Max felt like he'd been punched in the chest.

149

Olivia! In the Otherworld! At the same time, he had a terrible feeling that there was something very wrong, that there was something he knew that was important, but he couldn't remember it. The enchantress who stole away the Cornish prince — that had been Lady Morgana. Only King Arthur believed his half-sister's story that it was another witch in disguise. What was going on?

"But — it can't be — how ... What are we going to do?"

"We are going to rescue her," said another voice, firmly, and Max realized that there was someone else in the room — tall and dark and pacing up and down with fierce energy. It was the king. That would explain Merlin's careful choice of words.

At that moment the door opened, and Sir Bertram strode in, loaded with swords, armour, shields and helmets.

"Right then," he said. "Got everything we need. When do we set off?"

He looked over and saw that Max was awake, and

immediately dropped all the armour with a clatter and came over to the side of the bed.

"Max, m'boy," he said, and Max thought he had never seen his father look so grey or drawn. "Don't worry. We're going to get her back. Arthur's promised. And Merlin's coming. So we'll be fine."

Max sat up and saw that Caradoc was there, too, sitting at the foot of the bed, his long crooked face looking concerned. Adolphus was curled up by his feet with Ferocious, who scampered up to Max's shoulder and nipped his ear.

"It's my fault, Max. I went to get her. Heard all the commotion in the room and thought you needed help. And whatever they say," he added in a whisper, "it was Morgana in there, I'm sure of it . . ."

"Lady Morgana has promised to keep the way open for us," said Arthur to Sir Bertram. "Luckily she has also managed to locate the Cauldron of Annwn — so we have the payment for Olivia's life. She's frantic with worry about the poor girl — feels as if it's all her fault."

"It is," said Ferocious, and Merlin gave him a sharp look, but no one else in the room seemed to have heard him.

"She says she will prepare the spell and be ready for us tomorrow night," continued Arthur. "So we have time to make plans."

Merlin exchanged glances with Caradoc, and then cleared his throat.

"I have a suggestion. This . . . ah . . . enchantress, will be aware of our plans to rescue Olivia. She may try to prevent it, or . . . worse. If Lady Morgana opens the way, our going will be quite . . . public. I think we would do better to go tonight, quietly, with no one knowing but ourselves. Caradoc can open the way and hold it for us."

Arthur gave Merlin a piercing look, but Merlin returned it, his grey eyes meeting Arthur's blue ones and holding them steadily. At last Arthur nodded. "It is a sensible precaution. So. We will go tonight."

"The song says that seven only may return," said Caradoc. "Seven exactly, for the seven challenges. If

152

I am holding the way, and Olivia is to come back with you, then six will have to go. And it should be six who have a good reason, some connection to her."

"Well, that's me then," said Sir Bertram quickly. "And Arthur's a relative. And Merlin — well — he's a friend of the family . . ."

"So the other three will just have to be me, Ferocious and Adolphus," said Max. "And don't tell me we can't because we're coming, whatever anyone says."

"Yes, yes!" said Adolphus, jumping up from the bed. "We have to go. We have to rescue Olivia. We'll save her — we will!"

"Or die in the attempt," added Ferocious firmly. "Which we probably will. But we're not getting left behind, and that's that."

To the Rescue!

It was cold and windy on the hillside. The moon was full, but wisps of cloud kept floating across it. They could only see the vague shapes of the trees nearby and the looming bulk of the hill above them. They were standing by a small cave, and Caradoc was weaving little silvery spells across the entrance. Arthur was beside him, wearing armour and carrying his long sword, Excalibur. Merlin, looking grim, was similarly armed, and Sir Bertram was next to Max, telling him for the tenth time that he was to stay close, not wander away and on no account get himself killed. Max was clutching the cauldron Great-Aunt Wilhelmina had given him, wrapped up in a cloak, replacing the one Morgana had given Arthur. "Keep it safe, Max," Merlin had said as he switched the cauldrons over. "Something tells me that it came to you — and that you must be the one to return it."

As Caradoc stepped back from the cave entrance, they could all see the small silvery outline of a door glowing in the darkness.

"So," said Arthur. "It is time. Six of us go forth; seven shall return. Look out for us, Caradoc — we shall be back before dawn."

"We'll have to be," said Merlin. "At dawn the spell is broken and we won't be able to get back at all."

"We'll be here, don't worry," said Sir Bertram, gruffly. "Griselda would never let me hear the end of it, otherwise."

And one by one they strode through the glowing doorway, Max with Ferocious perched on his shoulder and Adolphus, who was quieter than usual, at his feet.

As Max walked through the silvery outline of the door, it felt as if he were wading into the sea; it was hard to walk and there was pressure all around him. Then he suddenly passed through to the other side, from night into day. A pale sun was burning through Annwn's early morning mist, dew was sparkling on the grass and ahead of them was a frothing, bubbling stream of jet-black water.

"Ah," said Merlin, heavily. "I had hoped this would not be the first challenge."

Arthur turned to him and frowned. "And this is?"

"The Stream of Jet," said Merlin. "It's an enchanted river. We can cross it if I make a magic bridge — but I can only do this once, and it will fail if I am not here, keeping the spell going. I'm afraid this is where I must stop and wait for your return."

"Great," said Ferocious. "We've only just got

here and we've lost the one person who knows what they're doing."

Arthur turned to Max and raised one eyebrow. "You know, Max, Merlin once spent a whole summer turning me into various strange creatures — with the useful result that I can now understand animal speech . . . So, Ferocious, rest assured, Merlin is not the only person here who knows what he's doing."

Ferocious squeaked and burrowed himself into Max's tunic in embarrassment, and Arthur laughed. His laughter was strong and clear and it made his face look younger, his blue eyes sparkling with amusement. Max found himself laughing, too, and it made him feel braver and bolder and sure that they were going to find Olivia and come home safely.

Merlin was standing by the stream, looking casually at the other bank. Now he turned and beckoned to them.

"All right," he said. "Go over as swiftly as possible once the bridge is made. There are six more tests, one for each of you and the last for Olivia. You must come back as quickly as you can. Don't get distracted — time is not quite the same in this land and it may pass more swiftly than it seems. Good luck!"

He gestured toward the stream, and there it was — a small wooden bridge, arching over the water, looking entirely solid and somehow very much like Merlin: deceptively plain, but strong, reliable and with a twist of bright magic running through every plank. Crossing over it, Max felt as if some of Merlin's strength and magic were passing into him with each step. And it was just as well they were, because Merlin's words had left him feeling rather apprehensive. A test for each of them? For him and Ferocious *and* Adolphus? How on earth were they supposed to know what to do when it was their turn? And what if they were last, and they didn't have Arthur or Sir Bertram to help them? Max bit his lip and tried not to think about it as he stepped off the bridge and onto firm ground on the other side.

It seemed like they walked through meadows and over rough pasture for hours without seeing anyone or anything. There was an eerie silence around them, and although the day seemed bright and clear, it was somehow hard to see any great distance. Sir Bertram, in full armour, was starting to get hot and fed up.

At last he stopped.

"Sorry, but I've had enough," he said. "It's about time we met someone."

He looked all around, and then cupped his hands and roared out at the nothingness.

"Come on! We've come to get Olivia! Come and stop us! Come and fight! Sneaks! Cowards! Come out and fight us!"

Arthur looked amused.

"Maybe you're right," he said, and added his voice to Sir Bertram's.

"It is I, High King Arthur of Britain, who calls you to a challenge. We seek Olivia Pendragon. Bring her to us, or face our swords!"

A ringing silence greeted these words, but then they heard a rattle of stones ahead. And, as they walked forward, suddenly a huge fortress loomed in front of them — a fortress that looked entirely solid and yet hadn't been there a moment before.

As they looked at it, the door in front of them creaked open and a servant beckoned them inside. She was small and slight, and had pale skin and merry green eyes that sparkled as she looked at each of them in turn.

"Welcome," she said, in a musical voice, "to the Fortress of Grog Insobriety."

They walked into a long hall and saw tables laden with jugs of grog and a feast of amazing food — roast swan, boars' heads, pastries and cakes and fruit, piles and piles of it. Around the tables were people dressed in bright colours, making merry and drinking and eating and dancing to wild music.

"One of you must stay," said the servant, and suddenly she looked more like a lady, dressed in finery, her long red hair braided with silver. "He must eat and drink and make merry until you return. Then, if he is still standing, you may collect him —

but if he falls, overcome with grog, he must remain. And then there will not be seven to pass over the bridge back to the kingdom of Britain."

They all looked at each other, and Sir Bertram coughed apologetically.

"Er . . . well . . . it looks like this one's mine, then. Knight Who Can Quaff the Most Grog and all that . . . Do my best."

He turned to Max and looked at him solemnly.

"Make sure you come back with Olivia, Max. I know you can do it." And he clapped him on the back, saluted Arthur and allowed the lady to lead him over to the tables.

At once the rest of them found themselves outside the fortress, back on the long, winding path through the Otherworld, and as Max looked up at the sky he realized it was already midday.

Bright though the overhead sun was, it was still impossible to see further than a few hundred yards in any direction. It wasn't that there was a mist, just that somehow it was hard to make your eyes focus

on the distance. They just slid over things and didn't quite register what they were. So it was a shock when, after another hour or so of tramping on along the path, Max suddenly realized that there was a crowd of people in front of them. People who seemed to have appeared out of nowhere. They were tall, and they were wearing long floaty dresses, and they all had long shining hair down to their waists.

"The Nine Maidens," said Arthur, and he smiled. "Now, I wonder whose challenge this is?"

The maidens looked at him, and simpered, and pouted, and ran their lily-white hands through their hair. They started to glide toward the group, eyes only for the king, with his tall frame and dark good looks, and Arthur found it hard not to return their smiles. He took his hand off the hilt of Excalibur, where it had rested almost since they'd entered the Otherworld, and reached out toward them as they approached.

"Hang on," said Max. "I don't think that's such a good idea."

But Arthur was walking forward as if entranced,

and he didn't seem to hear anything Max said.

"Well," said Ferocious, poking his head out and surveying the scene. "I think this one must be mine."

He slipped out of Max's tunic, scampered over the grass toward the maidens and started to bite their ankles.

At once they started to shriek, pull up their skirts and run around hopping and jumping to try and get away from the rat, who was like a small whirlwind of teeth and claws. And suddenly they didn't seem quite so beautiful or alluring. Ferocious drove them along the path until they reached a low flattish boulder onto which all nine climbed and then stood there, hissing with rage, while he circled the edge of the stone, baring his teeth at any of them who tried to come down.

King Arthur clapped his hands and bowed to Ferocious.

"I think we are now even," he said, looking slightly pink. "I am afraid I nearly made a very big fool of myself."

Ferocious grinned. "Well, I think we'll forgive you. Luckily beautiful maidens are not my sort of thing at all. Except for their nice plump ankles," he added, as one of them tried to put her foot down. She shrieked and whipped it out of the way.

"Go on then, quick," said Ferocious to the others. "I'll keep them here till you get back. But get a move on, won't you? It looks like it's mid-afternoon already."

Max looked at the sun. Ferocious was right. Time was definitely running faster here than at home. And they still had to find Olivia and be back by Annwn's sunset, which would signal dawn in their own world. Arthur nodded.

"You and me, now, Max."

"And Adolphus," Max reminded him. Adolphus had been very subdued ever since they'd entered the Otherworld. His tail was tucked down low and he'd barely said a word. He looked up now and licked Max's hand, but he didn't look happy.

Max hoped that Adolphus's challenge wouldn't

involve having to think too much.

They strode forward and almost instantly found themselves in a forest, with huge trees that seemed to reach up forever and disappear into a cool green darkness above them. There were no gleams of sunlight, and the forest floor was soft with layer upon layer of dead rotting leaves. They walked on in silence and then, faintly, Max heard a baying sound.

He turned to Arthur, who was also listening hard.

"Hounds," said the king at last, looking worried. "The hell hounds — the Hounds of Annwn — the Wild Hunt. They are supposed to be huge and fierce and each one has three heads . . . I think maybe this one is for me."

He drew Excalibur and stood, gesturing Max behind him, facing the sound of baying as it drew gradually nearer.

Now they could hear the crack of dry branches trampled underfoot, the rustle of undergrowth pushed aside by heavy bodies and the pant and roar of huge beasts as they came on through the forest. Then, there they were. Seven huge dogs — black as night, with white teeth, each with three heads — crouching together as if ready to spring, their eyes focused on Arthur and the bright sword in his hand.

Max's Task

The dogs stood there snarling, teeth bared, muscles tensed to spring. There was a pause, a moment of stillness, and then Adolphus threw himself forward joyfully and breathed an enormous flame of orange-red fire. He turned and leapt sideways, crouched and leapt again, and then hurled himself right up to the dogs shouting, "Whoopee! Let's play! Can't catch me! Come and try!" and tore off through the trees with all seven slavering dogs tearing after him.

"Flame and thunder!" said Arthur. "I thought my last hour had come. Good old Adolphus." He laughed with relief, clapped Max on the back and sheathed Excalibur.

Max could see glimpses of blue-green scales flashing in and out of the trees, and dark shadows following, around and around. The hounds were doing their best, but Adolphus had wings and he loved nothing more than a good game of chase. He was running rings around them. As Max watched, he saw one hound leap at Adolphus, all his teeth bared — but the dragon dodged, and the hound smacked straight into a tree and knocked two of his heads out cold. Max laughed.

"I think it's going to be all right," he said. "But we'd better get on. Probably supper-time already."

They left the wood and started trudging up a long hillside. Max could see that the sun was now quite low in the sky and he started to feel horribly anxious. It was getting late — and there was still his own challenge left to face. What if he couldn't do it? What if everyone managed theirs except him and it was his fault they all got stuck in Annwn forever?

Arthur looked down at him and squeezed his shoulder.

"You know, Max — I think there was a purpose behind each of us coming. I think there is a challenge for each person and it's the right one for them. When you meet yours, you'll know what to do. I trust you." His blue eyes were steady as he looked down at Max, and Max nodded, and swallowed hard.

At that instant a great castle of glass appeared in front of them, and standing by the drawbridge was a tall figure, dressed in black armour, with a huge sword.

"Now this one really *is* mine," said Arthur with a grin, and he drew Excalibur. "Go on, Max. Don't stop — I'll be waiting for you. You and Olivia."

He started to walk slowly toward the sentinel of the glass castle, who waited silently, his sword raised.

The sun was even lower now. Max didn't dare waste time waiting to see what happened when Arthur and the silent knight met. He heard a clash of swords behind him as he hurried forward, but he didn't look back.

So it's just me now, he thought, and he tried to run through the challenges Caradoc had outlined when they'd been preparing. The Nine Maidens, the Stream of Jet, the Fortress of Grog Insobriety — they'd gone past all of those. Then the Hounds of Annwn — Adolphus's friends. Arthur was facing the Silent Sentinel of the Castle of Glass. So that left . . . Max waggled his finger in his ear and tried to remember . . . The Flaming Door, he thought. The Flaming Door and . . .

The Brindled Ox.

It was the Brindled Ox. He could see it now, in front of him, head lowered, its wide, wicked horns stretching out impossibly far from each side of its massive head. It regarded him with liquid brown eyes, and although it didn't appear to make any noise, he heard a rumbling voice in his head:

"You may not pass."

The ox was standing in the middle of a strip of swampy marshland, with the gleam of dark water visible between clumps of marsh grasses. Only one narrow causeway led over the swamp, and the ox stood four-square in the middle of it, its great bulk outlined against the reddening sky.

Max gulped. He couldn't do this. He was terrible with animals. He was scared of horses, and even more scared of cows. There was no way he could get past this enormous bull, but if he didn't they'd never find Olivia, and none of them would get back alive.

He wondered if he could go around it. But the swamp looked very . . . well . . . swampy. He moved cautiously toward it, a close eye on the ox, and pushed his toe over the edge. It sank deep into the sticky, oozy mire. A terrible smell of decay wafted up to Max's nose and he nearly gagged. It was worse than the Great Grimpen Mire . . .

Suddenly he stood stock-still. What had he said

to Olivia? "When I'm sucked down to my death in the Great Grimpen Mire it will be all your fault ..." That was the day he hadn't wanted to miss lessons, the day they learned ... *how to make a swamp solid*! Max nearly whooped in glee as he realized that he could get across the swamp after all. He could bypass the huge ox completely!

He felt in his belt pouch for the small packet of powder he'd taken away from the lesson that day and took a deep breath. He sprinkled a few grains of purple powder over the swamp and muttered the words of the spell. And then he punched the air in triumph. Because, in front of him, the oozy mud was gradually turning dark and solid, and cracks were appearing as water was sucked away, until a clear path started to emerge right across the stretch of swamp.

Max turned and bowed to the huge ox, which nodded its great head and watched impassively as Max ran across the swamp and threw himself up the slope on the other side yelling, "Olivia! Olivia! I'm coming!"

As he reached the top of the slope and looked down, he stopped. He'd forgotten the final challenge. The Flaming Door. But there it was. Not so much a Flaming Door as a flaming everything. The door bit was the only part of the hillside that was not on fire.

***

Olivia was fizzing with impatience. When Morgana's spell had touched her, she had felt as if she'd been picked up by a whirlwind and then deposited gently on a grassy slope. Behind her was a gleaming wall of ice, in front of her a raging wall of flame. In the middle of the flame was a small dark opening through which she could see grass on the other side — but it was very small, and about waist height. Olivia didn't think she'd fit through it, even if she could bring herself to dive through head first. Beside her on the grass sat a white rabbit, its nose twitching.

"Where am I?" she said to the rabbit.

"Annwn," said the rabbit, and twitched its nose again.

"What should I do?" she asked.

"Nothing. Wait to be rescued," said the rabbit. It began to nibble at the grass, and then looked up. "Shouldn't be too long. They're at the river already."

"I'm not waiting to be rescued," said Olivia crossly. "I'll do my own rescuing, thank you!"

"I wouldn't recommend it," said the rabbit. "Anyway, they're on their way. Your father's just got to the drinking bit. Should be amusing . . ."

Olivia frowned. The rabbit twitched its nose and nibbled some more grass.

"Oh, do sit down," it said, after a while. "The Nine Maidens have failed — really, can't stand up to one rat between them. Pathetic. Let's hope the Hell Hounds do better."

Olivia sat down thoughtfully. It sounded like Ferocious was in the rescue party. She wondered if that meant Max was coming as well. She looked at the hole in the flaming wall and narrowed her eyes.

It hardly seemed five minutes before the rabbit looked up, twitched its nose again, said, "Ah, well, here he comes," and disappeared. The next second she could hear Max's voice, and then there he was, on the other side of the wall of fire, his anxious face peering through the hole.

"Olivia! Are you there?"

She stood up. "Max! Well done! You got here! Now we just have to get me through the wall!"

"Um, yes," said Max. "But I've got no idea how."

"Luckily, I have," said Olivia, who'd been thinking hard while she sat waiting. "The frogspell, Max — have you got the bottle?"

Max felt in his belt pouch. Yes, it was there. But there was hardly any left.

"I don't know if there's enough for both of us," he said doubtfully.

"Doesn't need to be," called Olivia. "Just chuck it through to me."

Max looked at the hole and measured his throw carefully, then hurled the bottle through. Olivia breathed a sigh of relief as it came through cleanly without touching the sides. Max didn't have the best aim in the world. Rapidly she uncorked the bottle and looked at the small drop of potion left in the bottom. Was there enough? She upturned the bottle over her head and shook it and — yes! — the world around her started to shiver, and get bigger . . . and there she was, a bright purple frog, just as she'd hoped.

Olivia looked carefully at the small hole surrounded by flames, flexed her back legs and leapt. She flew through the gap and landed on the grass right next to Max, who scooped her up and kissed her froggy head.

WHOOSH!!!

She was a girl again, her short dark hair sticking out, her green eyes dancing merrily, grinning hugely at Max. She punched him on the arm, and he grinned back, and held up the cauldron he'd carried all the way.

"Come on then! We need to hurry. Time is a bit strange in this place, and we've got to collect everyone and get back with this before Annwn's sun sets."

First up was King Arthur, and as they

approached the glass castle they could hear the great clash of swords and the panting of the two men, still fighting hard. They rounded the corner and saw Arthur, battle weary, his movements slow and painful, parrying the sentinel's blows again and again as the black knight pressed him back toward the edge of the drawbridge. He saw Max and Olivia approaching and rallied, swinging Excalibur high and bringing it crashing down on the knight's shield. But the knight barely flinched, and now Arthur was down, and the knight had raised his sword . . .

But Olivia had not spent four weeks practising Knock Down the Dummy With a Well-Aimed Saddlebag for nothing. She grabbed the cauldron from Max and hurled it. It whacked the black knight squarely on the helmet and sent him staggering sideways. It was all the chance Arthur needed, and within seconds the sentinel was on the ground, Excalibur at his throat and he yielded.

"Thank you, Olivia," said Arthur, taking off his helmet and wiping the sweat out of his eyes. "An unorthodox method of winning a fight, but I think you just saved my life."

Olivia went pink and tried to look nonchalant, while Max ran over to pick up the cauldron.

"Come on!" he said urgently. "I think we might have to run!"

They ran. In the forest, Adolphus joined them, bouncing joyfully. The Hell Hounds were all lying on the ground, their tongues lolling out, looking completely exhausted. They were covered with bruises and cuts from hurling themselves against the trees, and they barely managed to open one eye between the lot of them as Max and the others hurried past. As they reached the Nine Maidens, still stuck on their boulder with their skirts pulled up around their knees, Ferocious leapt onto Max's shoulder.

"Tail and whiskers!" he said thankfully. "I'm glad you made it. I was getting very tired of all their shrieking..."

Only a few minutes later they were at the

entrance to the Fortress of Grog Insobriety. There, swaying gently but still standing tall, was Sir Bertram, jug in one hand, pheasant leg in the other.

"Ah, there you are!" he greeted them. "Jolly good! Just in time . . . Feeling a bit woozy . . ."

Arthur grabbed one arm, and Max the other, and they marched Sir Bertram off down the path, keeping one anxious eye on the gleaming red sun, dipping low by the horizon.

"Come on! Come on!" called Adolphus, frantically running ahead and then back and then ahead again. "Just down here! Nearly there!"

And there they were. They could see the tall figure of Merlin standing by the bridge. He was silhouetted against the red sunset, and the black rushing waters of the river ran churning between them under the wooden arch of the bridge.

They started onto the bridge, but there was something stopping them from getting across — it was like a shimmering wall of glass. Arthur pushed angrily at it, but he could not get through. Merlin was gesturing at them, but no sound came across the rushing river. The sun had sunk still further now and was only a semi-circle visible against the dark horizon, wreathed in streaks of red and orange and gold. Sir Bertram threw himself at the wall, but it would not yield.

Suddenly Max realized that he was still holding the cauldron.

"The payment!" he shouted. "The Treasure of Annwn. We can't get across until we pay!"

Without hesitation, he hurled the cauldron into the icy black waters of the river. It floated for a second, then it slowly turned over and filled with water before sinking down, tumbling in the rush of water, and disappearing downstream. The shimmering wall melted away and they hurled themselves over the bridge. Together they ran through Caradoc's silvery doorway, just as the last gleam of the setting sun became the first gleam of dawn in their own world, on the side of a hill in the misty lakeland of Gore.

Songs and Celebrations

Of course, Morgana was furious when she discovered that Olivia had been rescued and everyone had returned safely.

She threw a vase at Sir Richard Hogsbottom's head, and blasted a fiery stream of white-hot magic at Snotty's back as he hurriedly retreated from her chambers. By deftly sidestepping, he just avoided being transported upside down to the castle dung heap.

However, she was all smiles when she came down to the Great Hall to greet the returning adventurers, and she congratulated Arthur on his successful quest with every appearance of sincerity.

"So *marvellous* to see the dear girl back — how *funny* that she was here all the time disguised as a boy and I never *realized*. Mordred tells me she's really quite good at squire training, for a girl." And she gave Olivia a little pat on the head, looking rather as if she were patting a slug.

Olivia went red, and Arthur said quickly, "Well, Morgana, I expect she's pretty good at squire training for a boy, as well. I think she probably saved my life with a well-aimed cauldron last night."

"Did she indeed?" said Morgana. "Well done!" She smiled at them as if she were chewing on lemons and then ushered them all toward the tables for a "welcome home" breakfast.

Sir Bertram, unusually for him, declined further food and went straight to bed with a sore head. But the others tucked in with a will, and they spent the rest of the morning exchanging stories and explaining all their adventures to anyone who would listen. In the end, Caradoc turned the whole story into a song and sang it to everyone, to great applause.

The rest of the week passed swiftly. Morgana left Aleric to run the Spell School, retiring to her chambers with a headache that lasted the entire week. The king used the time to visit some of the more far-flung corners of his kingdom and inspect the border forts. Unfortunately, while he was there, Sir Richard Hogsbottom made such a desperate plea to be sent back down south, away from the swamps and mud and mosquitoes, that Arthur gave in and recalled him to Camelot, much to Merlin's disquiet.

"That means Snotty will be in Camelot when we're there for the Squires' Challenge," said Max gloomily to Olivia. "We can't seem to get rid of him!"

"Never mind," she said with a grin. "Look on the bright side. All the more opportunities for turning him into a frog. Or, Max, you're going to be learning some new spells. Maybe you can find out how to turn him into a dung beetle!"

"Oh yes," said Ferocious. "A very appropriate insect. And much less likely to get kissed by anyone except another dung beetle."

It was the final Feast Day at the end of the Spell School, and Max and Olivia were seated at a long table in the Great Hall, tucking into a magnificent spread. Max had passed his Spell School exams, even with his old cauldron playing up slightly toward the end of the week. Luckily he'd managed to persuade Aleric that he'd misheard his instructions, and really did think he was supposed to turn the snail into a rhubarb pie, rather than make it fly. And Aleric had kindly overlooked the fact that Max's invisibility potion appeared to have the strange side effect of giving the invisible person hiccups. So Max now had his Certificate of Spell Mastery, and he was all set to start wizard training. Sir Bertram, who had been in a spectacularly good mood ever since they'd returned from Annwn, had promised he'd take Max and Olivia to Camelot when they got back. It would soon be September, and that was the time for the Annual Festival of Chivalry, always a good opportunity for a bit of drunken revelling and tales of daring around the fire. More importantly, it included the Squires' Challenge, which he was secretly beginning to think Olivia might just win. And besides, Merlin had suggested that it would be a good opportunity to look for a tutor for Max.

"Says in the meantime he'll teach you a bit himself," said Sir Bertram, clapping Max on the shoulder. "Bit of an honour, eh, Max? Most powerful wizard in the kingdom and all that. Seems quite impressed with you, I must say."

Max took a huge bite of venison pie and thought happily of lessons with Merlin. Maybe he *would* teach him how to turn people into dung beetles. How useful would that be! He grinned at Olivia and waved his flagon of apple juice in the air.

"Here's to Camelot and wizard lessons, and to you winning the Squires' Challenge!" he said.

She waved her flagon joyfully back.

"I don't even have to pretend to be a boy!" she said. "Arthur told Dad he'd accept me as a contestant because I'd proved my worth in Annwn. Isn't he brilliant?" She looked across the hall at where Arthur was laughing with some of his knights. She was glad to see that the king was not showing the slightest bit of interest in Lady Marianne the Fair, pouting nearby. He looked up, caught Olivia's eye and winked. Olivia thought she would happily die for him.

There was a stir and a bustle as Caradoc made his way into the hall with his harp, and to general acclaim started to sing the Lay of Annwn, the song he'd made up about King Arthur's adventures in the Otherworld.

"Good, isn't he?" came a voice from behind them, and Max turned to see Merlin standing in the shadows, watching Caradoc with an odd smile.

"He sings really well," said Max. "But he's not really a bard, is he?"

Merlin looked down at Max and Olivia and

seemed to hesitate for a second. Then he sat down beside them and shook his head.

"Well, not exactly," he said, in a low voice. "He and I have been working together for a while. Trying to stop Morgana's plots, trying to catch her out. It's been very hard to get proof, and Arthur insists on absolute, unquestionable proof before he will move against her. But we have been getting much nearer since you two came along. I think you've brought us luck, and a little magic of your own."

Max looked up at Merlin's hawk-like face and saw that he was smiling warmly. But Max felt slightly guilty.

"I'm not sure I helped, really. If I hadn't been so stupid Morgana wouldn't have been able to send Olivia to Annwn and then Arthur wouldn't have had to go there at all."

Merlin shook his head. "Morgana would have found a way to send someone there, don't worry, and Arthur would have been obliged to go once she'd let everyone know she had the Cauldron of Annwn. He can never resist a challenge, and wouldn't allow anyone to think he was a coward. She knew that when she made her plans. But you foiled the most important bit of the plot. We'd never have got back from that place without the real cauldron — the cauldron the dragon chose to give to you. Besides — there was your swamp spell! And not forgetting that Olivia only got through the Flaming Door with the help of your marvellous frogspell potion!" He laughed, and clapped Max on the back. "No, Max — I knew it was a good idea to ask you to keep an eye on Morgana while you were here. And I'm looking forward to having you around in Camelot for some serious magic lessons!"

Max felt a bubble of excitement at the thought of those magic lessons — with the most powerful wizard in the kingdom. He looked over at Caradoc, who'd taken his bow and then been forced to start the song all over again. The firelight illuminated his long crooked face and his large brown hands as he plucked the strings of his harp.

"He looks more like a knight than a bard," observed Olivia.

"He is a very able knight, one of the best," said Merlin. "And a dab hand at magic, too. When we've finally seen off the threat from Morgana, I think he'd like to join Arthur's little band of knights — and then they'll be in for a surprise. I've never met anyone yet who could beat him in a sword fight."

"What's his real name?" asked Max, curious.

Merlin hesitated, then nodded. "I think he'd be happy for me to tell you. We'll all be seeing a lot of each other one way or the other over the next few months. His real name . . . is Lancelot."

Max looked over again at the bard, and Caradoc looked up and caught his eye. He looked like he'd probably guessed what Merlin had been saying, because he smiled wryly, and half bowed to them all, and then carried on tunefully with the story of how Olivia's masterly throw had vanquished the Silent Sentinel of the Castle of Glass, and saved the life of the king.

About the author

C. J. Busby lived on boats until she was sixteen, and remembers one terrifying crossing of the English Channel in gale-force winds, when her family's barge nearly overturned. She spent most of her childhood with her nose in a book, even when walking along the road. Luckily she survived to grow up, but she still carried on reading whenever she could. She currently lives in Devon, Great Britain, with her three children and borrows their books whenever they let her.

Coming soon . . .

Max and Olivia's third hilarious adventure!

C. J. BUSBY
ILLUSTRATED BY DAVID WYATT

All is well in Camelot — not only is Max having magic lessons with the great wizard Merlin, Olivia is finally in training for the Squires' Challenge!

But disaster strikes when Camelot is frozen inside a magical mountain of ice and it's all Max's fault . . . Can he and Olivia rescue Arthur and Merlin from their icy prison before evil Lady Morgana gets to Camelot and seals their doom?